PENGUIN CLASSICS

THE SHADOW-LINE

JOSEPH CONRAD (Józef Konrad Korzeniowski), the only son of a leader of the abortive 1863 Polish revolt against Russian rule, was born in the Polish Ukraine in 1857. He passed his childhood in a Tsarist detention camp, and his adolescence in the old Polish capital of Cracow. Orphaned at an early age, he decided to go to sea in 1874, serving his apprenticeship from Marseilles, but establishing his career in the British Merchant Navy where, in 1886, he obtained his Master's certificate and British citizenship. After twenty-one years' varied and adventurous service, mostly in the Far East, he published his first novel, *Almayer's Folly*, married Jessie George, and, wholly changing his life for the second time, settled in Kent to become a professional writer. By the time of his death in 1924 he had produced a body of work which placed him in the front rank of English literature as one of the masters of early modernism. Many of his narratives are inspired by his sea career, but his work as a whole offers a far-ranging diagnosis of the political and moral crises attending the final phase of European expansionism.

JACQUES BERTHOUD was born in Switzerland and educated in Geneva and Johannesburg. He has taught at the Universities of Natal, Southampton and York, where he is now head of the Department of English and Related Literature. His more recent publications include *Joseph Conrad, the Major Phase*, and an edition of *The Nigger of the 'Narcissus'*.

THE SHADOW-LINE

A CONFESSION

JOSEPH CONRAD

EDITED WITH AN INTRODUCTION AND NOTES BY

JACQUES BERTHOUD

PENGUIN BOOKS

PENGUIN BOOKS

Published by the Penguin Group
27 Wrights Lane, London w8 5tz, England
Viking Penguin Inc., 40 West 23rd Street, New York, New York 10010, USA
Penguin Books Australia Ltd, Ringwood, Victoria, Australia
Penguin Books Canada Ltd, 2801 John Street, Markham, Ontario, Canada l3r 1b4
Penguin Books (NZ) Ltd, 182–190 Wairau Road, Auckland 10, New Zealand

Penguin Books Ltd, Registered Offices: Harmondsworth, Middlesex, England

First published 1917
Published in Penguin Books 1986
Reprinted 1987

Introduction, Bibliography and Notes copyright © Jacques Berthoud, 1986
All rights reserved

Made and printed in Great Britain by
Richard Clay Ltd, Bungay, Suffolk
Filmset in Monophoto Photina

CONTENTS

INTRODUCTION

AUTOBIOGRAPHY AND WAR

I

Of the works composed by Conrad during the First World War, *The Shadow-Line* is the only one that can be said to engage with that conflict. Yet it does so with such obliqueness that this has passed almost unperceived. The only critic to address this matter directly – Edward Said – was pressed by a thesis into imposing on the narrative a theory of allegorical autobiography that does little justice to its suggestive precision.[1] Otherwise commentary, from the first reviews to the latest exegetical exercise, has virtually ignored it. Yet all the evidence is that Conrad himself was particularly concerned that the wider significance of his story should not be overlooked. The very first sentence of the Author's Note he wrote in 1919 for the Collected Edition contains a warning that it is 'in its brevity a fairly complex piece of work' (p. 39). Moreover, its title pages are equipped with an elaborate apparatus of signals to the reader. The mysteriously evocative title, which positively invites interpretation, is supplied with a subtitle: *A Confession*; with a motto: 'Worthy of my undying regard';[2] with an epigraph: '*D'autres fois, calme plat, grand miroir / De mon désespoir*';[3] and, most strikingly, with a dedication: 'To Borys and all others who like himself have crossed in early youth the shadow-line of their generation, with love.' Taking Conrad at his word, I propose to consider the tale in the light of each of these, beginning with the last.

The dedication explicitly associates something outside the narrative – the enlistment of Conrad's eldest son as a second-lieutenant – with something inside it – his own appointment to his first command twenty-seven years earlier. And it does so with special poignancy, for the son's joining up and the father's reminiscences were almost exactly contemporaneous. On 15

November 1914, having barely extracted himself and his family from Poland, where the outbreak of war had marooned them, Conrad recorded that 'Borys [was] intensely miserable at not being yet of the serviceable age'. while he – Conrad – was 'painfully aware of being crippled, of being idle, of being useless'.[4] On 3 February 1915, he told his agent James Pinker that he was embarking on a story called *First Command*, a subject he had had in mind since 1899.[5] On 24 June he reported – erroneously as it turned out – to the same correspondent that he was expecting to finish in a few days. Meanwhile, Borys had made up his mind to enlist, even though he was still only seventeen, and on 20 September he was granted a commission in the Mechanical Transport Corps. Once again Conrad deplored his impotence: 'I am nearly driven distracted by my uselessness.'[6] In November he learnt that, contrary to his expectations, Borys's transfer to France was imminent; and on 17 December. after three months of sustained writing. he finished the tale he now called *The Shadow-Line.*

Whatever it may do, this summary does not encourage us to pursue the implications of the tale, as Said tends to, in analogies between the conduct of the plot and Conrad's military views, or between the ordeal of the protagonist and the fate of Europe.[7] On the contrary, Conrad seems to have registered the impact of the catastrophe, at least initially. through its effect on his son, identifying with him, in his paternal pride and envy, by means of his memories of a former self. He was acutely aware that this identification, taken the wrong way, might appear shockingly disproportionate. A few weeks before the novel's independent publication (it had first appeared in serial form), he expressed fears that the work might be dismissed as mere story-telling: 'I am really quite jumpy about the thing, and I think I'll cancel the dedication.'[8] Three years later, he was still as sensitive: 'Nobody can doubt that before the supreme trial of a whole generation I had an acute consciousness of the minute and insignificant character of my own obscure experience. There could be no question of any parallelism ... But there was a feeling of identity, though with an enormous difference of scale ...'[9] This difference, of course, was not only numerical but intensive. By the time he wrote these words he had been through the anguish of a parent with a son under arms, for Borys had participated in the Battle of the Somme, been swallowed up in the final German counter-offensive, and come out of the armistice gassed and shell-shocked.

But he did not remove the dedication and, with it, the book's claim to be regarded as a war novel. Yet in what sense can it be so regarded? For at least two inviting interpretative roads have been blocked: allegory (political or historical) and parallelism (between the two ordeals). A third possibility, however, is hinted at: 'there was a feeling of identity'. It seems clear that he regarded the *writing* of The Shadow-Line as an act of solidarity with the youthful combatants with whom he could no longer serve. The Author's Note offers an amplification of this idea: 'For when we begin to meditate on the meaning of our own past it seems to fill all the world in its profundity and its magnitude' (p. 40). This famous sentence has been taken to refer to the magnifying glass of nostalgia. But he tells us plainly that it is the *meaning* of the past, rather than its mere recollection, that seems to fill the world. If The Shadow-Line is a novel touched by war, it is less for the events it dramatizes than for the significance it discovers in them.

II

Unfortunately this distinction between events and meaning is not yet adequate to Conrad's conception of his novel, for he goes on to prevent us from drawing the obvious conclusion that 'what happened' doesn't matter. All the available evidence confirms that the subtitle, *A Confession*, is no mere decorative flourish. In fact, the outbreak of war seems to have undermined his confidence in the seriousness of fiction. On 28 January 1915, he wrote: 'It seems almost criminal levity to talk at this time of books, stories, publication.'[10] Again, on 11 August, he declared: 'Reality as usual beats fiction out of sight.'[11] Two years later he was still of the same opinion, insisting that The Shadow-Line be published by itself because 'I did not like the idea of its being associated with fiction in a vol. of short stories'.[12] Such, indeed, was his determination to insulate this work from the taint of 'invention' that it led him to exaggerate its fidelity to the facts, claiming it to be 'exact autobiography' on at least half a dozen occasions.[13] Nor is this impulse difficult to understand, for he was living through a period that endorsed all too clearly the truth that, however men might choose to fantasize their lives, they die in earnest, not in jest. He acknowledged as much to his friend Sidney Colvin when he told him that the 'exact truth' of his work was 'the reason I've dedicated it to Borys – and the Others'.[14] The uncompromising reality to which *they* were exposed seemed to require an equal renunciation on his part. Hence he offered *The Shadow-Line* not as the artistic elaboration of a fiction, but the artistic rendering of a fact.

But what kind of fact? This question is forced upon us by the researches of Norman Sherry who, in what is perhaps the most valuable chapter of *Conrad's Eastern World*, has been able to achieve a remarkable reconstruction of the circumstances surrounding Conrad's first command.[15] He demonstrates in detail the veracity of Conrad's account of Singapore and Bangkok, recovering the originals of the persons, places, incidents, itineraries and chronologies evoked by the novel. He also establishes beyond doubt that it cannot be treated as a historical record, for it manipulates and intensifies a number of crucial episodes – notably the craziness of the first mate, the villainy of the dead captain, and the affliction of the crew. How, then, can the claim of 'exact autobiography' be allowed to stand?

The answer resides in Conrad's conception of autobiography, which can be established from his correspondence with Colvin for this period of his career. Colvin had questioned his qualifications to review *The Shadow-Line* on the grounds that he lacked knowledge of the sorts of fact dug up by Norman Sherry. In reply, Conrad drew his attention to the subtitle, and explained: 'My object was to show all the others and the situation through the medium of my own emotions.' His aim was not self-disclosure, but committed perception. Such autobiography cannot be called 'subjective', for it does not project a pre-established self; nor can it be called 'objective', for it does not seek to reproduce a ready-made world. The exactness is fidelity to an existential apprehension of the world. Conrad attempts to clarify this in a passage which I am certainly not the first to try to interpret.

'But as a matter of fact all my concern has been with the "ideal" value of things, events and people. That and nothing else. The humorous, the pathetic, the passionate, the sentimental *aspects* come in of themselves – *mais en vérité c'est les valeurs idéales des faits et gestes humains qui se sont imposés à mon activité artistique* [but in truth it is the ideal values of human facts and actions that imposed themselves on my artistic activity].'[16] The question, of course, is what force to give to the phrase 'ideal values'. It is used attributively of objects of perception – of the things, events and people that make up the substance of his narration; it cannot therefore mean 'moral ideals' or even 'the fundamental principles that guide people in their actions'. Furthermore, the 'ideal values' of things are distinguished from their emotive effects, which are regarded as incidental: to apprehend something through the medium of an emotion (Conrad's earlier formulation) is not the same as reacting emotionally to it. The phrase seems to me analogous to the term 'tactile values' in painting. In the novel, things are not left to their neutral devices, or reduced to their practical or scientific 'values', but raised, in the plenitude and perfection of their being, to their 'ideal value'. But this presumes an autobiographical mode of perception: their vividness is a function of the intensity of the life that beholds them.

Consider the following case, which I draw from Conrad's greatest political essay, 'Autocracy and War'. Wars – particularly the carnage of modern warfare – take place because we are habitually too supine to imagine what they are really like or to believe that they could really happen to us. Even information about an actual conflict fails to move us. The 'vaunted eloquence' of statistics (of casualties, for instance) 'has all the futility of precision without force'. As for journalism, it is nothing more than a farce of knowledge: 'The printed page of the Press makes a sort of still uproar, taking from men both the power to reflect and the faculty of genuine feeling; leaving them only the artificially created need of having something exciting to talk about.' Only the 'direct vision of the fact' or the 'stimulus of great art' can open our eyes to the real meaning of war.[17] And even then, our saving callousness may soon teach us to 'assent to fatal necessity', or to submit to 'a purely esthetic [*sic*] admiration of the rendering'. From this point of view 'reality' is, paradoxically, an 'ideal' value difficult to achieve or to retain.

The autobiographical *Shadow-Line* is not in this respect essentially different from the fiction of a novelist whose credo was: 'Imagination, not invention, is the supreme master of art as of life.'[18] Conrad never relinquished his commitment to an artistic *conscience* (the legacy of a determinate history) limiting the play of invention to what it could make real to itself. Thus his best work was never allowed to cut free from an originating reality, whether in the form of recollection or of documentation. His art as a whole was designed to engage with a conception of life as resistance – as that which resists our illusions. The characteristic Conradian scenario is a test of the mind's constructions – of Jim's dream of heroism by the actual emergency, of Gould's project of regeneration by concrete material interests, of Heyst's pose of self-sufficiency by the fact of plurality. In that sense, his work was always on a potential war-footing. In 1914, however, the text had to be mobilized. It was no longer enough to say, 'I can imagine what a real ordeal is like': it became necessary to affirm, 'I survived an ordeal that actually took place.' The text became a sworn witness of the qualities needed to confront the crisis. It turned the autobiographical foundation of much of Conrad's art into a principle of justification. The art no longer merely interpreted the life; the life endorsed the art, permitting it to offer surrogate service in its identification with the combatants.

The problem with such a claim is that it can only be represented indirectly, for positive evidence that biographical fact supports fictional truth can only exist outside the work. Conrad was conscious of this difficulty, for he remarks in the Author's Note that the success of his first command left 'a tangible proof in the terms of the letter the owners of the ship wrote to me two years afterwards' (p. 41). Yet *The Shadow-Line* is not without corroborative indications, two of which can be found in its declared confessional form. The first is that the entire narrative is addressed directly to the reader. In sharp contrast to Conrad's usual practice, the authorial voice is not displaced by one or several narrators addressing a fictional audience, or enmeshed in irony-generating devices, like the Chinese boxes of 'Heart of Darkness', the mirrors of 'The Secret Sharer', or the random calendar of *A Personal Record*. To be sure, the autobiographer is necessarily divided from the autobiography, but we are never left in any doubt that he is Conrad learning to become Conrad. The second is that the tone of the narration is confidently natural from beginning to end. Its language inhabits a temperate region between colloquialism and artifice; in its clarity, sobriety, energy and ease, it is systematically unaffected and spontaneously controlled. Even the vocabulary of seamanship, which in a novel like *The Nigger of the 'Narcissus'* is deliberately underscored to contrast with the phraseology of symbolism, remains unobtrusively precise and integrated.

In a letter to a friend which accompanied the gift of a copy of *The Shadow-Line*, Conrad wrote: 'Absolute sincerity, I begin to think, is not natural to man; it's acquired by a long training in self-confidence.'[19] Clearly, the confessional integrity of his novel is an ideal achievement, sustained by tensions and contradictions that are everywhere apparent in his anterior work. Like Ransome's perfect courtesy, it is nourished by the knowledge that mankind dwells in enemy territory. Conrad's special strength comes from the fact that he made art out of a suspicion of art. *The Shadow-Line*, which is nothing if not a school of reality, was achieved out of something even more radical – the denial of art by the catastrophe to which it owes its existence.

III

The motto of *The Shadow-Line* – 'Worthy of my undying regard' – is at once a tribute to the ship's company and the announcement of a major narrative value: the interdependence of men. What bearing this has on Conrad's conception of war can be suggested by briefly returning to 'Autocracy and War'. This essay, which considers the implications of the Russo-Japanese conflict of 1904–5, attributes Japanese superiority less to the military arts than to the morale of the people ('since each people is an army nowadays'). Unlike the Russian soldiery which (in Conrad's view) has been contemptuously dragged out of a national void and hurled into an incomprehensible carnage, the 'Japanese army has for its base a reasoned conviction; it has behind it the profound belief in the right of a logical necessity to be appeased at the cost of so much blood and treasure'. Thus it is able to stand 'on the high ground of conscious assent, shouldering deliberately the burden of long-tried faithfulness'.[20] Rightly or wrongly, it has a principle of action which is also a principle of common identity, because it can command voluntary commitment and measure the required sacrifice. Conrad is silent about the content of this principle: his concern is with its effect. And in this he was perfectly consistent. Nothing is more striking in his correspondence after 1914 than his imperviousness to anti-German propaganda and his contempt for pro-British manifestos ('the democratic bawlings of our statesmen at Mme Germania'[21]). As he explained to an American friend: 'Here we don't fight for democracy or any other "-cracy" or for humanitarian or pacifistic ideals. We are fighting for life first, for freedom of thought and development in whatever form next.'[22] For him the war was simply a struggle for the survival of an independent nation of people.

The Shadow-Line is an attempt to explore, under very reduced conditions, the nature of this principle. Its protagonist, the young Conrad (for so he can be called, in deference to the subtitle), is taught that he could not have survived the ordeal to which he is exposed without a full reciprocity of dependence between himself and his crew. This lesson may seem banal enough; yet Conrad shows that it supports the entire edifice of human life.

Consider the novel's notoriously problematic opening. Without being able to explain why, or making alternative arrangements, the young first mate throws up a perfectly satisfactory berth. Now this impulsive act should not in itself have provoked critical consternation. It is intelligibly presented as an effect of 'the greensickness of late youth' (p. 45) – the natural pause in life when the sense of novelty begins to fade without the prospect of a compensatory meaning. But it can scarcely be justified as evidence of the young man's commitment to his career. Nor does his subsequent conduct in the Officers' Sailors' Home inspire more confidence. Acutely on the defensive, he locks the door on himself, treating those left outside with the inattention and indifference of moral contempt. This stance of self-sufficiency, of course, only serves to deliver him into the hands of others, whether they be malevolent, as with the chief steward, who tries to intercept the letter offering him the command, or benevolent, as with Captain Giles, who rescues him from this plot. The real puzzle is why this sort of behaviour should not have discredited him with his professional superiors.

He is, of course, an excellent seaman, instantly distinguishable from such failed sailors as the paranoiac chief steward or the self-infatuated Hamilton. As his response to the sight of his sailing-ship will shortly indicate, the commitment of competence is not his problem. But it remains surprising that not one of the father-figures who watch over his promotion regard his resignation in any way as a disqualification. The august harbour-master Ellis has no doubt that he is adequate to a difficult assignment. His former captain, Kent, gives him a first-class reference and sympathizes with his case. As for the maritime consultant Giles, he expends inexhaustible patience in coaxing him into a post which in his obtuseness he seems set on missing.

This problem will continue to breed critical abstractions until the first movement of the narrative is accepted as more than a preamble to the real business of the novel. It is a first and necessary stage in the general inquiry into how to survive an emergency. The novel provides a demonstration that success requires more than sheer professionalism – indispensable as that is. Or, more accurately, to be a good professional, you have to be more than professional. Under normal conditions, fidelity to the technicalities of the craft will see you through; but in an exceptional trial, it needs to be supplemented by human qualities that may have nothing to do with professional skills, and may even work against them. The idea of a double qualification slightly out of line with itself is not new in Conrad. In 'The Secret Sharer', for example, public and private obligation do not perfectly match: the narrator's commitment to a self that exists outside the boundaries of duty simultaneously endangers and enhances the self that exists within the terms of professional competence. In *The Shadow-Line*, however, this human surplus, so to speak, is more intimately bound to the responsibilities of command. It consists in the capacity to appeal, beyond the exactions of disciplined service, to the affection and loyalty of a ship's company. But such an appeal would be out of the reach of a man who conceived of service solely in terms of efficiency.

From this point of view, the young Conrad's resignation indicates that he wants more out of life than the satisfaction of disciplined progress. In fact his almost comic inability to see that a command is his for the taking exonerates him from vulgar ambition. And although his impulsiveness initially takes a self-regarding form, Giles – whose avuncular kindness, extended no less to the despairing chief steward than to the wayward young ex-mate, is an extra-professional bonus – seems to treat it as an inchoate virtue, or more specifically as independence in process of evolution. Certainly, when his opportunity comes, the petulant defiance disappears, if not immediately (for there remains a trace of it in his attitude to the captain who is taking him to Bangkok), then as soon as he joins his ship. And this is not because the appointment removes a grievance, but because it allows him to rise to itself.

The significance of this 'human surplus', as I have called it, is brought out by his treatment of his first mate Burns, who regards himself as an unsuccessful rival. When Burns is hospitalized with cholera, his new captain has every reason to leave him to his fate. He is indeed sensibly advised to delay his departure until he can secure a competent replacement. But with characteristic indiscretion he has him brought back on board. And this time there can be no doubt why he does so: the man, in his weakness, has appealed to him in the name of their common profession ('You and I are sailors'), and he finds this appeal irresistible. This decision, of course, greatly increases his difficulties in handling the ship; but it also eventually restores a good sailor to health and sanity ('I am very proud of him,' he declares at the end of the voyage) and, more important, it affirms the reality of professional comradeship, to which he owes above all else his success in coming out of the ordeal. The contrast offered by the conduct of his predecessor, whose personal disintegration reaches final expression in an outburst against his first officer – 'If I had my wish, neither the ship nor any of you would ever reach a port' (p. 89) – is equally instructive. This is nothing less than a blasphemy against the spirit of maritime solidarity, and it has a profoundly demoralizing effect on Burns. But it also entails a collapse of professional scruples, for, as his successor shortly discovers, he has sold the ship's stock of quinine to gratify his appetites in the flesh-pots of Haiphong.

To join professional discipline to the reciprocity of comradeship may involve some risk, for they are subject to different laws; but it is a risk that has to be taken. No man, even if he turns himself into a martinet of virtue, is able to stand alone. To be sure, as the pressures on him gradually become almost intolerable, the young Conrad is steadied by the training he has internalized: 'I was like a mad carpenter making a box. Were he ever so convinced that he was King of Jerusalem, the box he would make would be a sane box' (p. 120). But this is a desperate affirmation, which is in any case conditional on his being on deck. And this he ultimately owes not to his training, but to his readiness to seek and receive purely human support. When the immaculately constant Ransome, the ship's cook and steward, enters the cabin with the news that the crisis is at last upon them, he can scarcely endure the thought of the effort that awaits him. After a pause he says: ' "You think I ought to be on deck?" He answered at once, but without any particular emphasis or accent, "I do, sir." I got to my feet briskly . . .' (p. 126). And at the very same moment, in the next cabin, the half-crazed Burns is preparing the practically futile but morally telling gesture of coming up on deck too.

In a recent essay, Jeremy Hawthorn suggests that the young captain's remorse for not checking the quinine personally is exaggerated.[23] From a technical point of view, he is right: no court of inquiry could fail to accept the plea of a doctor's endorsement. But my argument has been that there exists in this tale another code, necessary to but independent of the first. And from that point of view the guilt he feels is a natural human response to the suffering of the men under his charge. This response is all the deeper for his recognition in them of the double imperative he has been discovering: 'I ask myself whether it was the temper of their souls or the sympathy of their imagination that made them . . . so worthy of my undying regard' (p. 120). Conrad's rendering of the spirit of that ship's company, when most of them are virtually dying on the job yet sustained by a subtle interplay of authority and companionship, is a triumph of the old writer's art celebrating the triumph of the young seaman's craft. And as the latter proves equal to the worst the sea can do. so the former declares its faith in a nation's capacity to survive the extremest trial of its history.

IV

As an oblique meditation on the significance of war. *The Shadow-Line* is centred on the nature of the ordeal it presents. Yet at once we are given pause. What connection can there be between a purely natural ordeal, like that of disease or dead winds, and the political affliction of military combat? Has not Conrad yielded to an irresponsibly fatalistic acceptance of what must continue to be. in principle at least, an avoidable evil?

If the First World War came as no surprise to him, it was not because of a dogmatic conviction of the essential belligerence of the human condition; but because of his political prescience. As early as 1905 he detected in the collision of industrial and commercial nationalisms every sign of a future disaster. He described their 'trust in the peaceful nature of this rivalry as 'an incredible infatuation', and predicted that 'democracy. which has elected to pin its faith to the supremacy of material interests, will have to fight their battles to the bitter end'.[24] Such a view is the reverse of stoical complacency, for it focuses attention on the moral consequences of folly and greed. But it is not compatible with moralizing on the event either; when it is on us, to glorify it or to denounce it is equally futile. It exists now; it has to be faced – either actively, as his son was able to do, or reflectively. as he himself was compelled to do, finding very little fatalistic repose in the evidence before him that the universe into which man has strayed leaves him entirely to his own devices. As he brutally wrote to Ford on 30 August 1915: 'Yes! *mon cher!* our world of 15 years ago is gone to pieces: what will come in its place. God knows. but I imagine doesn't care.'[25]

The indifference of nature to its strangest invention – human consciousness – is of course the Conradian theme *par excellence.* But the new challenge gives it a new emphasis, to which the novel's epigraph unobtrusively directs us. It is taken from a poem which compares music to the sea, but in a manner that makes it

difficult to distinguish vehicle from tenor. Its concluding metaphor
– the epigraph itself – repeats this dilemma at a different level. Is
the source of the despair inside or outside the speaker? How are we
to differentiate between the subjective and the objective, between
the self and what is outside it?

It has been widely recognized that the qualified affirmation with
which *The Shadow-Line* concludes is purchased at the cost of a
succession of disillusionments. But how, precisely, this process
ministers to its end is by no means evident. The young captain sees
the command that suddenly lights on him as the resolution of all
his incoherent discontents; his ship presents itself to him as a
promise of happiness, and he takes his place in the master's cabin
in all the security of dynastic succession. But he quickly discovers
that his inheritance is a poisoned one. He therefore contracts his
hopes, putting all his faith in the open sea as a release from the
physical, moral and commercial entanglements of land. Once at
sea, however, the weather fails, and the crew's illness persists: he
is reduced to concentrate what remains of his trust on the quasi-
magical properties of a medicinal powder. When even that prop
collapses, all he is left with is himself, stuck in a meteorological
emptiness. The process, then, is one that involves the self; but even
that formulation is not enough. For example, it is misleading to
suggest, as one of Conrad's most perceptive critics has just done,
that the young captain is made to discover 'identity as something
not given but (at least in part) still to be constructed'.[26] On the
contrary, what is required is its *de*construction.

Or rather, a dismantling of ready-made conceptions of the self.
Of the vacuity of such conceptions, Conrad had long been convinced. In a letter of 4 September 1892 to his aunt, who had
complained about a nephew's fecklessness, he wrote: 'One always
thinks oneself important at 20. The fact is, however, that one only
becomes useful when one realises the full extent of the insignificance of the individual in the arrangement of the universe.'[27] The
opening of the narrative reveals a young man enclosed in a cara-
pace of suspect confidence. He has, as we have seen, no doubt of
his fitness to pass judgement on the inmates of the Sailors' Home.
He even assumes a superiority of tone towards Giles, whose style
seems to him too commonplace to deserve unqualified respect. In

short, he strikes a morally heroic attitude (by no means to be confused with the performance of a heroic deed) which is found wanting, both by the tale itself, and by the great events under whose shadow it was written.

To be secure in one's identity is to be convinced that one is in full possession of 'a sound mind'. Commenting on one of his conversations with Giles he remarks: 'It never occurred to me then that I didn't know in what soundness of mind exactly consisted, and what a delicate and, upon the whole, unimportant matter it was' (p. 57). For the moment, however, the line dividing madness from sanity seems stable: he does not hesitate, for instance, to distance himself from the steward's 'craziness' – even when Giles warns him that 'everybody in the world is a little mad', himself not excepted (p. 74). But it is not to remain stable for long. Far from leaving the subject behind, the first thing he discovers when he joins his ship is that his predecessor has fallen apart mentally, and that his first mate is possessed by the demon of the dead captain. And, this time, he is no longer able to dissociate himself from what he continues to call 'craziness'. In fact he is increasingly drawn into it, and begins to lose his sense of what counts as a rational explanation. For example, the sudden glimpse of a pair of scissors in Burns's hand shoots into his mind the idea that his first officer is trying to cut his throat (a mark of final collapse) when he is only attempting to trim his beard (a hint of recovery). Indeed, the very violence with which he resists Burns's dogmatic attribution of the freak weather to a supernatural cause – the dead man's curse – suggests that he may be in way of catching the infection himself.

His experience of the dissolution of the rational self ('despair') is in exact coincidence ('mirror') with his discovery of the inertness of nature ('flat calm'). The two extracts from his diary record implicitly the sensations of a man who finds himself inhabiting a strictly senseless universe. What finally unsettles him is not the fact of adversity, but its mindlessness. The relentless alternation of identical days and nights, 'as if somebody below the horizon were turning a crank' (p. 117), transforms the world into a cosmic automaton. The fitful gusts of the disease on board mechanically replicate the random breaths of air expiring around the ship, and take away his command as effectively as they deprive his vessel of steerage. And as the world empties itself of life and sense, so thought and purpose begin to drain out of the self.

This converging double movement meets at the moment of crisis. A blinding darkness descends on the ship, marooning every man in a kind of nothingness. (When Conrad writes that 'there was in it an effect of *inconceivable* terror and of *inexpressible* mystery' (p. 126; my italics), he means exactly what he says, however unsatisfactory the phrasing may be to some of his critics.) While he is in this condition, the young captain stumbles over an 'animal shape', and is struck by a flash of superstitious panic. But the shape resolves itself into the familiar figure of the first mate, who has managed to drag himself up from below in order to defy the corpse at the bottom of the gulf.

This psychological and narrative resolution, which coincides with the long-delayed break in the weather, has proved to be the central exegetical problem of the tale. It turns on the degree to which the text itself (for *Conrad* repudiates such an interpretation in his Author's Note) might be said to endorse the supernatural explanation of the wind's return. But in the kind of universe that the tale has created, supernaturalism would be as much out of place as providentiality.[28] It has consistently associated superstition with a mad response to the world – a response with no more than the limited authority of being preferable, because better informed, than that of complacency and confidence. If the line between sanity and madness is a thin one, it is scarcely surprising that the distinction between a rational and a superstitious reading of the text should not be blatant. But, however indirect it may be, for Conrad a criterion of differentiation *exists* – not in what a man may feel, but in what he does. We have seen that he may not be able to achieve that state of grace by himself; but the point here is that both men – Burns hysterically defying the source of his hysteria, the young captain exorcizing his anguish in the discovery that it has a human cause – and with them the rest of the crew, confront the enemy within and are therefore able, when the chance at last presents itself, to bring the ship to port.

What is perhaps most impressive about *The Shadow-Line* is that it shows us men capable of acting not out of heroics but out of weakness. The pressure of war under which the novel was written makes itself felt in the discovery that what men are up against is not only ahead of them, but also inside their ranks. Without exception, every member of the ship's company is damaged or incomplete, whether afflicted by disease or by the emotional instability that is the penalty of self-consciousness. In short, they are fractured by the impersonal process that has created them in order to destroy them. Yet for all this, none of them – except perhaps the young 'cub' of a second mate – capitulates. On the contrary, the whole narrative is designed to affirm that only on the basis of a consciousness of weakness can the edifice of the human world be secured. Hence it is that Ransome, without whose unobtrusive perfection of conduct neither the captain nor his ship might have survived, becomes the novel's symbol and emblem; for unlike his comrades in suffering, who are granted remission, his malady is a congenital one which never lets him forget even for the moment of a heartbeat that he is mortal, and hence never allows him to compromise that decorum of self-possession which preserves and justifies his and our existence on earth.

Giles's valedictory remarks to the young Conrad, who has been reporting the story of his trial, seem to close the novel with a certificate of maturity: 'A man has got to learn everything' (p. 144). But this conclusion is that there is no conclusion: what has been learnt is that the lesson is never done. There is no point of rest, either in the past or in the future. Even here the resonance of war continues to be audible; for Conrad, who foresaw its advent, is warning us about its ending. And indeed, only a few short years were to pass before the novel proved prophetic. The closure of victory, the finality of virtue, the establishment of peace by the war to end war – these confident illusions imposed on him no more than had the propaganda of conflict. 'I'll confess that neither felicity nor peace inspire me with much confidence,' he wrote to Galsworthy on 24 December 1918. 'There is an air of the "packed valise" about these two ... figures.'[29] But not about The Shadow-Line, whose openness goes far to explain why, confined as it is to the world of men, it is not inaccessible to women, and why, limited to the context of an ordeal at sea, it permits the perception of a second, more tenebrous, context encompassing the first.

NOTES

1. Edward W. Said, *Joseph Conrad and the Fiction of Autobiography*, Harvard University Press, Cambridge, Mass. (1966), pp. 165–97.
2. *The Shadow-Line*, p. 120.
3. 'At other times, flat calm, great mirror / Of my despair,' from Baudelaire, *Les Fleurs du Mal*, in *Œuvres complètes*, Pléiade ed., Gallimard, Paris (1961), p. 65.
4. To Sir Ralph Wedgwood, in G. Jean-Aubry, *Joseph Conrad, Life and Letters*, Heinemann, London (1927), Vol. II, p. 162. Hereafter referred to as *LL2*.
5. Z. Najder, *Joseph Conrad: A Chronicle*, Cambridge University Press (1983), p. 407. Hereafter referred to as *Najder*.
6. To F. W. Dawson, 11 August 1915, quoted in *Najder*, p. 409.
7. For example, Said considers seamanship in *The Shadow-Line* to be an expression of Conrad's faith in 'Europeanism', and the 'decomposition' of the narrator a reflection of the disintegration of Europe. See Said, op. cit., pp. 189 and 192 respectively.
8. To. J. B. Pinker, *LL2*, p. 182.
9. Author's Note to *The Shadow-Line* p. 40.
10. To Lady Wedgwood, *LL2*, p. 189.
11. To F. N. Doubleday, quoted in *Najder*, p. 409.
12. To Sir Sidney Colvin, 27 February 1917 *LL2*, p. 183.
13. For example to J. B. Pinker, early 1917; to Sidney Colvin, 27 February 1917; to Helen Sanderson, 1917; *LL2*, pp. 181, 182 and 195 respectively.
14. 27 February 1917, *LL2*, p. 183.
15. Norman Sherry, *Conrad's Eastern World*, Cambridge University Press (1966), pp. 211–49.
16. To Sir Sidney Colvin, 18 March 1917, *LL2*, pp. 184–5.
17. 'Autocracy and War', *Notes on Life and Letters*, Dent Collected Edition, London (repr. 1949), pp. 84 and 90. This essay was written in Capri during the first three months of 1905, and printed in the *Fortnightly Review*.
18. *A Personal Record*, Dent Collected Edition, London (repr. 1960), p. 25.
19. To Christopher Sandeman, end of April 1917, *LL2*, p. 191.
20. 'Autocracy and War', pp. 87–8.
21. To Christopher Sandeman, 15 September 1917, *LL2*, p. 197.
22. To John Quinn, 6 May 1917, New York Public Library, quoted in *Najder*, p. 424.

23. In his Introduction to his edition of *The Shadow-Line* for 'The World's Classics', Oxford University Press (1985). p. xvii.

24. 'Autocracy and War', p. 107.

25. *LL2*, p. 169.

26. Hawthorn, op. cit. p. xi.

27. To M. Poradowska, 4 September 1892, in R. Rapin (ed.), *Lettres de Joseph Conrad à Marguerite Poradowska*, Droz, Geneva (1966), p. 102: 'On se croit toujours important a 20 ans. Le fait est cependant que l'on ne devient utile que quand on realise toute l'etendue de l'insignificance de l'individu dans l'arrangement de l'univers' [accentuation and orthography *sic*].

28. Conrad is explicit about this, as the following wryly detached comment makes clear: 'By the exorcising virtue of Mr Burns's awful laugh, the malicious spectre had been laid, the evil spell broken. the curse removed. We were now in the hands of a kind and energetic Providence' (p. 139). This is scarcely the tone of metaphysical reverence.

29. *LL2*, pp. 215–16.

SELECT CRITICAL BIBLIOGRAPHY

I have listed the following selection of critical essays in chronological order of accessible publication. The fact is that many appeared in journals considerably earlier than in book form, so that my list cannot be taken to offer an orderly profile of the debate. That I pass summary judgement against some of them does not imply that they should not have been written, of course, but that a *prise de position* is a necessary by-product of intellectual engagement.

1. Douglas Hewitt, *Conrad: A Reassessment*, Bowes and Bowes, Cambridge (1952), pp. 112–17.

   Like 'Typhoon', the novel gains in clarity of purpose and firmness of execution by accepting a limited scope: the achievement of unpretentious maturity through a straightforward test of courage and responsibility. Questions of 'fundamental good and evil' are put aside, and, with them, the 'lush' rhetoric and 'portentous' moralizing which mar the later work. This view is too simple.

2. Ian Watt, 'Story and Idea in Conrad's *The Shadow-Line*', *Critical Quarterly*, Vol. 2, no. 2 (1960), pp. 133–48.

   The classic essay on the novel. It establishes an important distinction between 'heterophoric' or allegorical interpretation, in which meaning is external to narrative, and 'homeophoric' or intrinsic readings which seek the enlarged significance of the given. Differentiating himself from Leavis and Guerard, who oppose too sharply the traditional code of duty and the instabilities of human experience (though coming to alternative conclusions), Watt discerns in the tale a revelation of the indifference of things which demands moral resistance as it exacts moral dissolution. The protagonist's victory, therefore, is not absolute, but dependent on the efforts of others, whether as an inheritance from the past, or as collaboration in the present. The conclusion is not triumphant, but qualified by sickness and death.

3. Norman Sherry, *Conrad's Eastern World*, Cambridge University Press (1966), pp. 284–90.

A synoptic survey of the novel. It is a folk-tale in which the hero, aided by 'good fairies', has to break the spell of evil enchantment; a factual tale based on the author's own experience; a tale of maturing through testing, and encountering a representative variety of men.

4. Albert Guerard, *Conrad the Novelist*, Harvard University Press (1966), pp. 29–33.

The novel is not about the temptation of the supernatural, nor the passage from youth to maturity, but about the experience of immobilizing depression first displayed in the 'seriously defective' first chapters, where the protagonist does not suffer from ignorant confidence but neurotic immobilization. It offers a journey into the night of the self which is discovered to be tripartite (symbolized by the irrational Burns and the rational Ransome at war within the anguished consciousness). Conrad may think he is writing about seamanship and maturity; but his real concern is with disintegrative melancholy. Although this critic's psychoanalytic verve is famous, one may wish to ask how its conclusions might or might not be falsified.

5. Thomas Moser, *Joseph Conrad: Achievement and Decline*, Archon Press, Connecticut (1966), pp. 137–43.

The affirmation that the novel offers is unconvincing, because the 'evil' that has to be faced is a purely external one: Ransome's disability is merely physical, the dead captain is at the bottom of the gulf, and the narrator is really guiltless (his guilt is merely a mental state). Although the judgement differs from Guerard's, the assumptions are in subtle accord.

6. Edward Said, *Joseph Conrad and the Fiction of Autobiography*, Harvard University Press (1966), pp. 165–97.

The novel is autobiographical in that it re-enacts Conrad's continuous struggle against dissolution, formerly as a seaman, now as a writer and an Englishman faced by incoherence and catastrophe. On these premises, Said weaves a web of elaborate analogies, of which the principal one is between the threatened break-up of the self and of Europe. Thus both are imprisoned in a terrible, futureless present; both must serve an impersonal ideal (seamanship-writing and 'Europeanism'); both will survive only by relying on 'doing', conceived communally. This attempt to project the novel as a sort of double allegory of Conrad's writing life and of the contemporary history of Europe seems to me to demand too tense a virtuosity in the performer; but it remains the only piece in the repertoire to confront the contextual dimension of the work.

7. F. R. Leavis, 'The Shadow-Line', in *'Anna Karenina' and Other Essays*, Chatto and Windus, London (1967), pp. 92–110.

This is the only essay on the work in which the *process* of response, discovery, confirmation and judgement is shown to be intrinsic to the critical act. At times almost holding a dialogue with himself, Leavis suggests that the drama of reading is at one with the drama of narrative. The result is a remarkably unalienated recognition of the maturity of the novel in its ironic demonstration that there is more to life than uncritical professionalism.

8. J. I. M. Stewart, *Joseph Conrad*, Dodd, Mead & Co., New York (1968), pp. 240–47.

The 'first third' is 'disastrously bad', and the writing, except for the description of the crisis, is slack. The narrator, obscurely aware that he must extend himself, is offered the desired test, the command being less a promotion than the gaining of a 'throne'. In contrast to the protagonist of 'The Secret Sharer', he has nothing to conceal, and is given the support of his crew. Conrad simply celebrates *'les valeurs idéales'*, i.e. heroism. A depressing exhibition of English common sense in action.

9. Lawrence Graver, *Conrad's Short Fiction*, University of California Press (1969).

After noting Conrad's alleged ambivalence towards autobiography and the supernatural, Graver produces a straightforward account of 'the education of a young egoist' caught between the altruism of Giles, the medical officer and Ransome, and the self-regard of the chief steward, the dead captain and Burns – all of which results in a cautionary optimism.

10. C. B. Cox, *Joseph Conrad: The Modern Imagination*, J. M. Dent, London (1974), pp. 150–58.

An efficiently humane though ultimately slightly reductive reading which advises us 'to settle down to cope with our own mediocrity'. Although the story only really comes to life when the captain joins his ship, its moral climax is blunted by Conrad's ambiguous treatment of the role of supernaturalism. Still, the story demonstrates that a commitment to positive values need not result in rhetoric or triviality.

11. Gary Geddes, *Conrad's Later Novels*, McGill-Queen's University Press, Montreal (1980), pp. 81–113.

A stylish but perhaps over-leisurely examination of virtually all aspects of the novel. The captain of *The Shadow-Line* suffers not from personal insecurity but disappointed idealism. Hence his problem is to rediscover a link between himself and the moral world, which he does at a new level, by integrating personal conduct into the tradition of continuity. He recognizes his own insignificance, his dependence on others, and the inconclusiveness of experience. This process, which enables Conrad to review his career of resistance to self-doubt and indifference, becomes a passionate defence of commitment to work. This story belongs to the late Conrad in that the obligations of comedy and romance, present in its formal structure, purge it of artifice.

12. D. R. Schwarz, *Conrad: The Later Fiction*, Macmillan, London (1982), pp. 81–94.

Like Geddes, Schwarz is firmly convinced of the redemptive virtue of work. The novel rejects the Baudelairean correspondence between the inner and the outer, distinguishing sharply between an objective maritime tradition and the subjective experience of captain and crew. Adherence to a received system of duty is the only means of controlling personal doubts and of resisting external pressures. Thus the protagonist's initial malaise is not a form of neurosis, but the 'boredom' experienced by the exceptional man in need of the imperatives of responsibility.

13. Jeremy Hawthorn, Introduction to *The Shadow-Line* (World's Classics), Oxford University Press (1985), pp. vii–xxv.

Hawthorn addresses a variety of relevant topics in a fresh and lively way. His edition is noteworthy for its inclusion of deleted passages from the manuscript, hitherto unpublished, in particular a 550-word account of a nightmare experienced by the narrator, which dramatizes the depth of his disturbance, though, I think, in terms of the anxieties of insecurity rather than of guilt. The introduction is striking for its quest for symbols: Christian (original sin), Shakespearean (Hamlet's 'surplus' guilt' and feminist (the female ship). That I have reservations about all of these (for example, the novel seems to me the reverse of anti-feminist not because the narrator likes his ship but because of his undogmatic, open conception of the self, and hence of the masculine gender) is not to imply that the questions raised are useless, and certainly not that the essay's human seriousness is irrelevant.

NOTE ON THE TEXT

The outline of the bibliographical history is as follows:

1. The manuscript was completed and dated on 15 December 1915. It is now in the Beinecke collection of the Yale University Library.

2. It was first published serially in a) the *English Review* over seven numbers from September 1916 to March 1917. and b) the *Metropolitan Magazine*, New York in October 1916.

3. It was first published in book form a) in London and Toronto by J. W. Dent in March 1917 (227 pp.), and b) in New York by Doubleday, Page in the same year (197 pp.), both without any prefatory material.

4. It was first published in a collected edition in 1920 by Doubleday, Page, New York, as the fifteenth volume (with *Within the Tides*) of the so-called 'Sun Dial' Edition, prefaced with an Author's Note. Duplicates of the plates were sold to J. M. Dent, and used for the Dent Uniform Edition of 1923–8. and for all subsequent collected editions, down to the Dent Collected Edition of 1945–50, reprinted several times.

5. It was also published in a first London collected edition of 780 sets by William Heinemann (1921–7) as their fourteenth volume (again with *Within the Tides* and with the Author's Note) in 1921. Thereafter the plates were distributed, and the edition had no successors. Conrad corrected the proofs, which have been preserved in the Rosenbach collection, Philadelphia.

I have not been able to examine either the manuscript or the corrected proofs, but Jeremy Hawthorn has compared photocopies of both with his copy-text, that of the Dent Collected Edition (i.e. the descendant of the 'Sun Dial'); and his findings are recorded in his 'World's Classics' edition (Oxford University Press, 1985). I have, however, thanks to the generous assistance of Mr Nicholas Barker, Head of the Preservation Service of the British Library, compared the texts of the Dent First Edition (1917), the Doubleday, Page 'Sun Dial' Edition (1920), and the Heinemann Collected Edition (1921); and I have had no hesitation in selecting the latter as my copy-text. The 'Sun Dial' is close to the Dent First (to the point of sometimes repeating its mistakes) and has the alleged attraction of reproducing its slightly lighter punctuation. But the Heinemann Collected is to be preferred because: a) it has the authority of Conrad's final corrections; b) it has, in my view, a more consistent and responsible house style; and c) all its alterations, except for those listed below, whether authorial or editorial, seem to me to clarify and focus the intentions of the language. I have made exception in the following five cases (DF: Dent First; SD: 'Sun Dial'; HC: Heinemann Collected):

p. 60, l. 26   He leaned against the lintel of the door] HC; lintel] DF; side] SD. I have accepted 'side' on the grounds that the gesture proposed by HC and DF presupposes powers of levitation.

p. 64, l. 23   after, perhaps, ninety days at sea] HC; after perhaps ninety] DF; after perhaps ninety] SD. I have omitted commas on the grounds that the thought seems spontaneous rather than speculative.

p. 114, l. 11   that it was, perhaps, just as well] HC; was perhaps just] DF; was perhaps just] SD. I have omitted the commas because, again, the qualification aimed at does not seem deliberative.

p. 126, l. 6   'Very black, indeed, sir] HC; black indeed,] DF; black indeed,] SD. I have omitted the comma, on the grounds that it weakens the colloquial emphasis.

p. 132,   while his judgment, his reason still tries to resist] HC
l. 16–17   still try] DF; still try] SD. Although this has the authority of Conrad's correction (Hawthorn), the punctuation does not suggest a single subject, but two subjects in apposition. I have therefore restored the text to Conrad's first thoughts ('try').

I have made one grammatical alteration:

p. 63, l. 12   was the crew] HC. This now reads 'were the crew'.

A minuscule crux (variants are all relatively trivial in this text) is worth noting:

p. 86,   He was a peculiar man – of sixty-five about – iron-
l. 25–26   grey, hard-faced] HC: of sixty-five about] DF: of about
           sixty-five] SD; of sixty-five about] ms (Hawthorn).
           Although it is tempting, with SD, to straighten out
           the odd locution, this would lose the colloquial energy
           so characteristic of Burns. I have therefore not altered
           the copy-text.

Of the several manuscript passages either omitted or altered in
the text of the first edition, by far the most substantial is the
following, which would have appeared at the end of Chapter III, p.
100, l. 7–8, after the words 'Enough to get under way with, he
said'. It is quoted in Lawrence Graver, *Conrad's Short Fiction*, University of California Press (1969), pp. 182–3:

I was oppressed by my lonely responsibility; weighed down by it in that
cabin, gloomy with the lamp turned down and where my predecessor had
expired under the eyes of a few awed seamen.

The passage of death made of it like a vast solitude. I took refuge from it
in my state-room where nobody had died as far as I knew. After all the
passion of anger and indignation I had thrown into my activities on shore
the unpeopled stillness of that gulf weighed on my shaken confidence like a
mere artifice of some inimical force – I upbraided myself for the very
existence of that unwholesome sensation. I resisted it. But that resistance
itself was a manifestation of a self-consciousness which was to me a strange
experience, distasteful and disquieting. I welcomed a great wave of fatigue
that all at once overwhelmed me from head to foot [in my] struggle against
morbidity.

Without taking off any of my clothing – not even removing my cap from
my head – I ensconced [sic] myself in the corner of the couch and crossing
my arms on my breast fell into a profound slumber.

I dreamt of the Bull of Bashan. He was roaring beyond all reason on his
side of a very high fence striking it with his forehoof and also rattling his
horns against it from time to time. On my side of the fence my purpose was
(in my dream) to lead a contemplative existence. I despised the brute,
but gradually a fear woke up in me that he would end by breaking
through –not through the fence – through my purpose. A horrible fear. I
tried to fight against it and mainly to keep it down with my hands. But it
got the better of me like a powerful compressed spring might have done –
violently.

I found myself on my feet, very scared by my dream and in addition
appalled by the apparition of the late captain in front of my open door. For

what else could be that dim figure in the halflight of the cuddy, featureless, still malevolently silent, not to be mistaken for anything earthly.

Before my teeth began to rattle however the apparition spoke in a hoarse apologetic voice which no ghost would have thought it necessary to adopt. Certainly not the ghost of that savage overbearing old sinner who would have liked to take his ship out of the world with him.

It was but the voice of the seaman on watch who had come down to tell me that there were faint airs off the land. Enough he thought to get underway with.

I told him to call all hands to man the windlass. Before he left the cabin it occurred to me to ask him whether he had much trouble to wake me up.

'You were very sound off Sir' he said with much feeling as he retired. That was it! He must have had to shout pretty loud. He was the Bull of Bashan of my dream, so detailed, so vivid, so concrete as to be more real than the great shadowy peace which met me when I came on deck.

THE SHADOW-LINE

A CONFESSION

'Worthy of my undying regard.'

AUTHOR'S NOTE

This story, which I admit to be in its brevity a fairly complex piece of work, was not intended to touch on the supernatural. Yet more than one critic has been inclined to take it in that way, seeing in it an attempt on my part to give the fullest scope to my imagination by taking it beyond the confines of the world of living, suffering humanity. But, as a matter of fact, my imagination is not made of stuff so elastic as all that. I believe that if I attempted to put the strain of the Supernatural on it it would fail deplorably and exhibit an unlovely gap. But I could never have attempted such a thing, because all my moral and intellectual being is penetrated by an invincible conviction that whatever falls under the dominion of our senses must be in nature and, however exceptional, cannot differ in its essence from all the other effects of the visible and tangible world of which we are a self-conscious part. The world of the living contains enough marvels and mysteries as it is – marvels and mysteries acting upon our emotions and intelligence in ways so inexplicable that it would almost justify the conception of life as an enchanted state. No, I am too firm in my consciousness of the marvellous to be ever fascinated by the mere supernatural, which (take it any way you like) is but a manufactured article, the fabrication of minds insensitive to the intimate delicacies of our relation to the dead and to the living, in their countless multitudes; a desecration of our tenderest memories; an outrage on our dignity.

Whatever my native modesty may be it will never condescend so low as to seek help for my imagination within those vain imaginings common to all ages and that in themselves are enough to fill all lovers of mankind with unutterable sadness. As to the effect of a mental or moral shock on a common mind, it is quite a legitimate subject for study and description. Mr Burns's moral being receives a severe shock in his relations with his late captain, and this in his diseased state turns into a mere superstitious fancy compounded of fear and animosity. This fact is one of the elements of the story, but there is nothing supernatural in it – nothing, so to speak, from beyond the confines of this world, which in all conscience holds enough mystery and terror in itself.

Perhaps if I had published this tale, which I have had for a long time in my mind, under the title of *First Command*, no suggestion of the Supernatural would have been found in it by any impartial reader, critical or otherwise. I will not consider here the origins of the feeling in which its actual title, *The Shadow-Line*, occurred to my mind.[1] Primarily the aim of this piece of writing was the presentation of certain facts which certainly were associated with the change from youth, care-free and fervent, to the more self-conscious and more poignant period of maturer life. Nobody can doubt that before the supreme trial of a whole generation I had an acute consciousness of the minute and insignificant character of my own obscure experience. There could be no question here of any parallelism. That notion never entered my head. But there was a feeling of identity, though with an enormous difference of scale – as of one single drop measured against the bitter and stormy immensity of an ocean. And this was very natural too. For when we begin to meditate on the meaning of our own past it seems to fill all the world in its profundity and its magnitude. This book was written in the last three months of the year 1916.[2] Of all the subjects of which a writer of tales is more or less conscious within himself this is the only one I found it possible to attempt at the time. The depth and the nature of the mood with which I approached it is best expressed perhaps in the dedication which strikes me now as a most disproportionate thing – as but another instance of the overwhelming greatness of our own emotion to ourselves.

This much having been said, I may pass on now to a few remarks about the mere material of the story. As to locality, it belongs to that part of the Eastern Seas from which I have carried away into my writing life the greatest number of suggestions.[3] From my statement that I thought of this story for a long time under the title of *First Command* the reader may guess that it is concerned with my personal experience. And, as a matter of fact, it *is* personal experience seen in perspective with the eye of the mind and coloured by that affection one can't help feeling for such events of one's life as one has no reason to be ashamed of. And that affection is as intense (I appeal here to universal experience) as the shame, and almost the anguish, with which one remembers some unfortunate occurrences, down to mere mistakes in speech, that have been perpetrated by one in the past. The effect of perspective in memory is to make things loom large because the essentials stand out isolated from their surroundings of insignificant daily facts which have naturally faded out of one's mind. I remember that period of my sea-life with pleasure because, begun inauspiciously, it turned out in the end a success from a personal point of view, leaving a tangible proof in the terms of the letter the owners of the ship wrote to me [4] two years afterwards when I resigned my command in order to come home. This resignation marked the beginning of another phase of my seaman's life, its terminal phase, if I may say so, which in its own way has coloured another portion of my writings. [5] I didn't know then how near its end my sea-life was, and therefore I felt no sorrow except at parting with the ship. I was sorry also to break my connection with the firm which owned her and who were pleased to receive with friendly kindness and give their confidence to a man who had entered their service in an accidental manner and in very adverse circumstances. Without disparaging the earnestness of my purpose I suspect now that luck had no small part in the success of the trust reposed in me. And one cannot help remembering with pleasure the time when one's best efforts were seconded by a run of luck.

The words, 'Worthy of my undying regard,' selected by me for the motto on the title page, are quoted from the text of the book itself; and, though one of my critics surmised that they applied to the ship, it is evident from the place where they stand that they refer to the men of that ship's company: complete strangers to their new captain, and who yet stood by him so well during those twenty days that seemed to have been passed on the brink of a slow and agonising destruction. And *that* is the greatest memory of all! For surely it is a great thing to have commanded a handful of men worthy of one's undying regard.

1920   J. C.

THE SHADOW-LINE

'. . . D'autres fois, calme plat, grand miroir
De mon désespoir.'[1]

BAUDELAIRE

CHAPTER ONE

Only the young have such moments. I don't mean the very young.
No. The very young have, properly speaking, no moments. It is the
privilege of early youth to live in advance of its days in all the
beautiful continuity of hope which knows no pauses and no intro-
spection.

One closes behind one the little gate of mere boyishness – and
enters an enchanted garden. Its very shades glow with promise.
Every turn of the path has its seduction. And it isn't because it is
an undiscovered country. One knows well enough that all mankind
had streamed that way. It is the charm of universal experience
from which one expects an uncommon or personal sensation – a
bit of one's own.

One goes on recognising the landmarks of the predecessors.
excited, amused, taking the hard luck and the good luck together –
the kicks and the halfpence, as the saying is – the picturesque
common lot that holds so many possibilities for the deserving or
perhaps for the lucky. Yes. One goes on. And the time. too. goes on
– till one perceives ahead a shadow-line warning one that the
region of early youth, too, must be left behind.

This is the period of life in which such moments of which I have
spoken are likely to come. What moments? Why, the moments of
boredom, of weariness, of dissatisfaction. Rash moments. I mean
moments when the still young are inclined to commit rash actions.

such as getting married suddenly or else throwing up a job for no reason.

This is not a marriage story. It wasn't so bad as that with me. My action, rash as it was, had more the character of divorce – almost of desertion. For no reason on which a sensible person could put a finger I threw up my job – chucked my berth – left the ship of which the worst that could be said was that she was a steamship and therefore, perhaps, not entitled to that blind loyalty which . . . However, it's no use trying to put a gloss on what even at the time I myself half suspected to be a caprice.

It was in an Eastern port.[2] She was an Eastern ship,[3] inasmuch as then she belonged to that port. She traded among dark islands on a blue reef-scarred sea, with the Red Ensign[4] over the taffrail[5] and at her masthead a house-flag, also red, but with a green border and with a white crescent[6] in it. For an Arab owned her, and a Syed at that.[7] Hence the green border on the flag. He was the head of a great House of Straits Arabs, but as loyal a subject of the complex British Empire as you could find east of the Suez Canal. World politics did not trouble him at all, but he had a great occult power amongst his own people.

It was all one to us who owned the ship. He had to employ white men in the shipping part of his business, and many of those he so employed had never set eyes on him from the first to the last day. I myself saw him but once, quite accidentally on a wharf – an old, dark little man blind in one eye, in a snowy robe and yellow slippers. He was having his hand severely kissed by a crowd of Malay pilgrims to whom he had done some favour, in the way of food and money. His almsgiving, I have heard, was most extensive, covering almost the whole Archipelago. For isn't it said that 'The charitable man is the friend of Allah'?[8]

Excellent (and picturesque) Arab owner, about whom one needed not to trouble one's head, a most excellent Scottish ship – for she was that from the keel up – excellent sea-boat, easy to keep clean, most handy in every way, and if it had not been for her internal propulsion, worthy of any man's love, I cherish to this day a profound respect for her memory. As to the kind of trade she was engaged in and the character of my shipmates, I could not have been happier if I had had the life and the men made to my order by a benevolent Enchanter.

And suddenly I left all this. I left it in that, to us, inconsequential manner in which a bird flies away from a comfortable branch. It was as though all unknowing I had heard a whisper or seen something. Well – perhaps! One day I was perfectly right and the next everything was gone – glamour, flavour, interest, content- ment – everything. It was one of those moments, you know. The green-sickness of late youth descended on me and carried me off. Carried me off that ship, I mean.

We were only four white men on board, with a large crew of Kalashes[9] and two Malay petty officers. The captain[10] stared hard as if wondering what ailed me. But he was a sailor, and he, too, had been young at one time. Presently a smile came to lurk under his thick, iron-grey moustache, and he observed that, of course, if I felt I must go he couldn't keep me by main force. And it was arranged that I should be paid off the next morning. As I was going out of the chart-room he added suddenly, in a peculiar, wistful tone, that he hoped I would find what I was so anxious to go and look for. A soft, cryptic utterance which seemed to reach deeper than any diamond-hard tool could have done. I do believe he understood my case.

But the second engineer[11] attacked me differently. He was a sturdy young Scot, with a smooth face and light eyes. His honest red countenance emerged out of the engine-room companion and then the whole robust man, with shirt-sleeves turned up, wiping slowly the massive forearms with a lump of cotton-waste. And his light eyes expressed bitter distaste, as though our friendship had turned to ashes. He said weightily, 'Oh, aye! I've been thinking it was about time for you to run away home and get married to some silly girl.'

It was tacitly understood in the port that John Nieven was a fierce misogynist; and the absurd character of the sally convinced me that he meant to be nasty – very nasty – had meant to say the most crushing thing he could think of. My laugh sounded de- precatory. Nobody but a friend could be so angry as that. I became a little crestfallen. Our chief engineer[12] also took a characteristic view of my action, but in a kindlier spirit.

He was young, too, but very thin, and with a mist of fluffy

brown beard all round his haggard face. All day long, at sea or in harbour, he could be seen walking hastily up and down the after-deck, wearing an intense, spiritually rapt expression, which was caused by a perpetual consciousness of unpleasant physical sensations in his internal economy. For he was a confirmed dyspeptic. His view of my case was very simple. He said it was nothing but deranged liver. Of course! He suggested I should stay for another trip and meantime dose myself with a certain patent medicine in which his own belief was absolute. 'I'll tell you what I'll do. I'll buy you two bottles, out of my own pocket. There. I can't say fairer than that, can I?'

I believe he would have perpetrated the atrocity (or generosity) at the merest sign of weakening on my part. By that time, however, I was more discontented, disgusted, and dogged than ever. The past eighteen months, so full of new and varied experience, appeared a dreary, prosaic waste of days. I felt – how shall I express it? – that there was no truth to be got out of them.

What truth? I should have been hard put to it to explain. Probably, if pressed, I would have burst into tears simply. I was young enough for that.

Next day the captain and I transacted our business in the Harbour Office.[13] It was a lofty, big, cool, white room, where the screened light of day glowed serenely. Everybody in it – the officials, the public – was in white. Only the heavy polished desks gleamed darkly in a central avenue, and some papers lying on them were blue. Enormous punkahs[14] sent from on high a gentle draught through that immaculate interior and upon our perspiring heads.

The official behind the desk we approached grinned amiably and kept it up till, in answer to his perfunctory question, 'Sign off and on again?' my captain answered, 'No! Signing off for good.' And then his grin vanished in sudden solemnity. He did not look at me again till he handed me my papers with a sorrowful expression, as if they had been my passports for Hades.

While I was putting them away he murmured some question to the captain, and I heard the latter answer good-humouredly:

'No. He leaves us to go home.'

'Oh!' the other exclaimed, nodding mournfully over my sad condition.

I didn't know him outside the official building, but he leaned forward over the desk to shake hands with me, compassionately, as one would with some poor devil going out to be hanged; and I am afraid I performed my part ungraciously, in the hardened manner of an impenitent criminal.

No homeward-bound mail-boat was due for three or four days. Being now a man without a ship, and having for a time broken my connection with the sea – become, in fact, a mere potential passenger – it would have been more appropriate perhaps if I had gone to stay at an hotel. There it was, too, within a stone's-throw of the Harbour Office, low, but somehow palatial, displaying its white, pillared pavilions surrounded by trim grass plots. I would have felt a passenger indeed in there! I gave it a hostile glance and directed my steps towards the Officers' Sailors' Home.[15]

I walked in the sunshine, disregarding it, and in the shade of the big trees on the esplanade without enjoying it. The heat of the tropical East descended through the leafy boughs, enveloping my thinly clad body, clinging to my rebellious discontent, as if to rob it of its freedom.

The Officers' Home was a large bungalow with a wide verandah and a curiously suburban-looking little garden of bushes and a few trees between it and the street. That institution partook somewhat of the character of a residential club, but with a slightly Governmental flavour about it, because it was administered by the Harbour Office. Its manager was officially styled Chief Steward.[16] He was an unhappy, wizened little man, who if put into a jockey's rig would have looked the part to perfection. But it was obvious that at some time or other in his life, in some capacity or other, he had been connected with the sea. Possibly in the comprehensive capacity of a failure.

I should have thought his employment a very easy one, but he used to affirm for some reason or other that his job would be the death of him some day. It was rather mysterious. Perhaps everything naturally was too much trouble for him. He certainly seemed to hate having people in the house.

On entering it I thought he must be feeling pleased. It was as still as a tomb. I could see no one in the living-rooms; and the verandah, too, was empty, except for a man at the far end dozing prone in a long chair. At the noise of my footsteps he opened one horribly fish-like eye. He was a stranger to me. I retreated from there, and, crossing the dining-room – a very bare apartment with a motionless punkah hanging over the centre table – I knocked at a door labelled in black letters: 'Chief Steward'.

The answer to my knock being a vexed and doleful plaint, 'Oh dear, oh dear! What is it now?' I went in at once.

It was a strange room to find in the tropics. Twilight and stuffiness reigned in there. The fellow had hung enormously ample, dusty, cheap lace curtains over his windows, which were shut. Piles of cardboard boxes, such as milliners and dressmakers use in Europe, cumbered the corners; and by some means he had procured for himself the sort of furniture that might have come out of a respectable parlour in the East End of London – a horsehair sofa, arm-chairs of the same. I glimpsed grimy antimacassars [17] scattered over that horrid upholstery, which was awe-inspiring, insomuch that one could not guess what mysterious accident, need, or fancy had collected it there. Its owner had taken off his tunic, and in white trousers and a thin, short-sleeved singlet prowled behind the chair-backs nursing his meagre elbows.

An exclamation of dismay escaped him when he heard that I had come for a stay; but he could not deny that there were plenty of vacant rooms.

'Very well. Can you give me the one I had before?'

He emitted a faint moan from behind a pile of cardboard boxes on the table, which might have contained gloves or handkerchiefs or neckties. I wonder what the fellow did keep in them? There was a smell of decaying coral, or Oriental dust, of zoological specimens in that den of his. I could only see the top of his head and his unhappy eyes levelled at me over the barrier.

'It's only for a couple of days,' I said, intending to cheer him up.

'Perhaps you would like to pay in advance?' he suggested eagerly.

'Certainly not!' I burst out directly I could speak. 'Never heard of such a thing! This is the most infernal cheek . . .'

He had seized his head in both hands – a gesture of despair which checked my indignation.

'Oh dear, oh dear! Don't fly out like this. I am asking everybody.'

'I don't believe it,' I said bluntly.

'Well, I am going to. And if you gentlemen all agreed to pay in advance I could make Hamilton [18] pay up too. He's always turning up ashore dead broke, and even when he has some money he won't settle his bills. I don't know what to do with him. He swears at me and tells me I can't chuck a white man out into the street here. So if you only would . . .'

I was amazed. Incredulous too. I suspected the fellow of gratuitous impertinence. I told him with marked emphasis that I would see him and Hamilton hanged first, and requested him to conduct me to my room with no more of his nonsense. He produced then a key from somewhere and led the way out of his lair, giving me a vicious, sidelong look in passing.

'Any one I know staying here?' I asked him before he left my room.

He had recovered his usual pained, impatient tone, and said that Captain Giles [19] was there, back from a Solo Sea [20] trip. Two other guests were staying also. He paused. And, of course, Hamilton, he added.

'Oh yes, Hamilton!' I said, and the miserable creature took himself off with a final groan.

His impudence still rankled when I came into the dining-room at tiffin-time.[21] He was there on duty overlooking the Chinamen servants. The tiffin was laid on one end only of the long table, and the punkah was stirring the hot air lazily – mostly above a barren waste of polished wood.

We were four around the cloth. The dozing stranger from the chair was one. Both his eyes were partly opened now, but they did not seem to see anything. He was supine. The dignified person next him, with short side-whiskers and a carefully scraped chin, was, of course, Hamilton. I have never seen any one so full of dignity for the station in life Providence had been pleased to place him in. I had been told that he regarded me as a rank outsider. He raised not only his eyes, but his eyebrows as well, at the sound I made pulling back my chair.

Captain Giles was at the head of the table. I exchanged a few words of greeting with him and sat down on his left. Stout and pale, with a great shiny dome of a bald forehead and prominent brown eyes, he might have been anything but a seaman. You would not have been surprised to learn that he was an architect. To me (I know how absurd it is) he looked like a churchwarden. He had the appearance of a man from whom you would expect sound advice, moral sentiments, with perhaps a platitude or two thrown in on occasion, not from a desire to dazzle, but from honest conviction.

Though very well known and appreciated in the shipping world, he had no regular employment. He did not want it. He had his own peculiar position. He was an expert. An expert in – how shall I say it? – in intricate navigation. He was supposed to know more about remote and imperfectly charted parts of the Archipelago than any man living. His brain must have been a perfect warehouse of reefs, positions, bearings, images of headlands, shapes of obscure coasts, aspects of innumerable islands, desert and otherwise. Any ship, for instance, bound on a trip to Palawan²² or somewhere that way would have Captain Giles on board, either in temporary command or 'to assist the master'. It was said that he had a retaining fee from a wealthy firm of Chinese steamship owners, in view of such services. Besides, he was always ready to relieve any man who wished to take a spell ashore for a time. No owner was ever known to object to an arrangement of that sort. For it seemed to be the established opinion at the port that Captain Giles was as good as the best, if not a little better. But in Hamilton's view he was an 'outsider.' I believe that for Hamilton the generalisation 'outsider' covered the whole lot of us; though I suppose that he made some distinctions in his mind.

I didn't try to make conversation with Captain Giles, whom I had not seen more than twice in my life. But, of course, he knew who I was. After a while, inclining his big, shiny head my way, he addressed me first in his friendly fashion. He presumed from seeing me there, he said, that I had come ashore for a couple of days' leave.

He was a low-voiced man. I spoke a little louder, saying that, No – I had left the ship for good.

'A free man for a bit,' was his comment.

'I suppose I may call myself that – since eleven o'clock,' I said. Hamilton had stopped eating at the sound of our voices. He laid down his knife and fork gently, got up, and, muttering something about 'this infernal heat cutting one's appetite,' went out of the room. Almost immediately we heard him leave the house down the verandah steps.

On this Captain Giles remarked easily that the fellow had no doubt gone off to look after my old job. The chief steward, who had been leaning against the wall, brought his face of an unhappy goat nearer to the table and addressed us dolefully. His object was to unburden himself of his eternal grievance against Hamilton. The man kept him in hot water with the Harbour Office as to the state of his accounts. He wished to goodness he would get my job, though in truth what would it be? Temporary relief at best.

I said, 'You needn't worry. He won't get my job. My successor is on board already.'

He was surprised, and I believe his face fell a little at the news. Captain Giles gave a soft laugh. We got up and went out on the verandah, leaving the supine stranger to be dealt with by the Chinamen. The last thing I saw they had put a plate with a slice of pine-apple on it before him and stood back to watch what would happen. But the experiment seemed a failure. He sat insensible.

It was imparted to me in a low voice by Captain Giles that this was an officer of some Rajah's yacht which had come into our port to be dry-docked. Must have been 'seeing life' last night, he added, wrinkling his nose in an intimate, confidential way which pleased me vastly. For Captain Giles had prestige. He was credited with wonderful adventures and with some mysterious tragedy in his life. And no man had a word to say against him. He continued:

'I remember him first coming ashore here some years ago. Seems only the other day. He was a nice boy. Oh, those nice boys!'

I could not help laughing aloud. He looked startled, then joined in the laugh. 'No, no! I didn't mean that,' he cried. 'What I meant is that some of them do go soft mighty quick out here.'

Jocularly I suggested the beastly heat as the first cause. But Captain Giles disclosed himself possessed of a deeper philosophy. Things out East were made easy for white men. That was all right. The difficulty was to go on keeping white, and some of these nice boys did not know how. He gave me a searching look, and in a benevolent, heavy-uncle manner asked point-blank:

'Why did you throw up your berth?'

I became angry all of a sudden; for you can understand how exasperating such a question was to a man who didn't know. I said to myself that I ought to shut up that moralist; and to him aloud I said with challenging politeness:

'Why . . .? Do you disapprove?'

He was too disconcerted to do more than mutter confusedly, 'I! . . . In a general way . . .' and then gave me up. But he retired in good order, under the cover of a heavily humorous remark that he, too, was getting soft, and that this was his time for taking his little siesta – when he was on shore. 'Very bad habit. Very bad habit.'

The simplicity of the man would have disarmed a touchiness even more youthful than mine. So when next day at tiffin he bent his head towards me and said that he had met my late captain last evening, adding in an undertone, 'He's very sorry you left. He had never had a mate that suited him so well,' I answered him earnestly, without any affectation, that I certainly hadn't been so comfortable in any ship or with any commander in all my seagoing days.

'Well – then,' he murmured.

'Haven't you heard, Captain Giles, that I intend to go home?'

'Yes,' he said benevolently. 'I have heard that sort of thing so often before.'

'What of that?' I cried. I thought he was the most dull, unimaginative man I had ever met. I don't know what more I would have said, but the much-belated Hamilton came in just then and took his usual seat. So I dropped into a mumble.

'Anyhow, you shall see it done this time.'

Hamilton, beautifully shaved, gave Captain Giles a curt nod, but didn't even condescend to raise his eyebrows at me; and when he spoke it was only to tell the chief steward that the food on his plate wasn't fit to be set before a gentleman. The individual addressed seemed much too unhappy to groan. He only cast his eyes up to the punkah and that was all.

Captain Giles and I got up from the table, and the stranger next to Hamilton followed our example, manœuvring himself to his feet with difficulty. He, poor fellow, not because he was hungry, but I

so on. He had felt out of sorts somewhat on rising. Nothing much. Just enough to make him feel lazy.

All this with a sustained, holding stare which, in conjunction with the general inanity of the discourse, conveyed the impression of mild, dreary lunacy. And when he hitched his chair a little and dropped his voice to the low note of mystery, it flashed upon me that high professional reputation was not necessarily a guarantee of sound mind.

It never occurred to me then that I didn't know in what soundness of mind exactly consisted, and what a delicate and, upon the whole, unimportant matter it was. With some idea of not hurting his feelings I blinked at him in an interested manner. But when he proceeded to ask me mysteriously whether I remembered what had passed just now between that steward of ours and 'that man Hamilton,' I only grunted sour assent and turned away my head.

'Aye. But do you remember every word?' he insisted tactfully.

'I don't know. It's none of my business,' I snapped out, consigning, moreover, the steward and Hamilton aloud to eternal perdition.

I meant to be very energetic and final, but Captain Giles continued to gaze at me thoughtfully. Nothing could stop him. He went on to point out that my personality was involved in that conversation. When I tried to preserve the semblance of unconcern he became positively cruel. I heard what the man had said? Yes? What did I think of it then? – he wanted to know.

Captain Giles's appearance excluding the suspicion of mere sly malice, I came to the conclusion that he was simply the most tactless idiot on earth. I almost despised myself for the weakness of attempting to enlighten his common understanding. I started to explain that I did not think anything whatever. Hamilton was not worth a thought. What such an offensive loafer . . . – 'Ay! that he is,' interjected Captain Giles – . . . thought or said was below any decent man's contempt, and I did not propose to take the slightest notice of it.

This attitude seemed to me so simple and obvious that I was really astonished at Giles giving no sign of assent. Such perfect stupidity was almost interesting.

'What would you like me to do?' I asked, laughing. 'I can't start a row with him because of the opinion he has formed of me. Of course, I've heard of the contemptuous way he alludes to me. But he doesn't intrude his contempt on my notice. He has never expressed it in my hearing. For even just now he didn't know we could hear him. I should only make myself ridiculous.'

That hopeless Giles went on puffing at his pipe moodily. All at once his face cleared, and he spoke.

'You missed my point.'

'Have I? I am very glad to hear it,' I said.

With increasing animation he stated again that I had missed his point. Entirely. And in a tone of growing self-conscious complacency he told me that few things escaped his attention, and he was rather used to think them out, and generally from his experience of life and men arrived at the right conclusion.

This bit of self-praise, of course, fitted excellently the laborious inanity of the whole conversation. The whole thing strengthened in me that obscure feeling of life being but a waste of days, which, half-unconsciously, had driven me out of a comfortable berth, away from men I liked, to flee from the menace of emptiness ... and to find inanity at the first turn. Here was a man of recognised character and achievement disclosed as an absurd and dreary chatterer. And it was probably like this everywhere – from east to west, from the bottom to the top of the social scale.

A great discouragement fell on me. A spiritual drowsiness. Giles's voice was going on complacently; the very voice of the universal hollow conceit. And I was no longer angry with it. There was nothing original, nothing new, startling, informing to expect from the world: no opportunities to find out something about oneself, no wisdom to acquire, no fun to enjoy. Everything was stupid and overrated, even as Captain Giles was. So be it.

The name of Hamilton suddenly caught my ear and roused me up.

'I thought we had done with him,' I said, with the greatest possible distaste.

'Yes. But considering what we happened to hear just now I think you ought to do it.'

'Ought to do it?' I sat up bewildered. 'Do what?'

Captain Giles confronted me very much surprised.

'Why! Do what I have been advising you to try. You go and ask the steward what was there in that letter from the Harbour Office. Ask him straight out.'

I remained speechless for a time. Here was something unexpected and original enough to be altogether incomprehensible. I murmured, astounded.

'But I thought it was Hamilton that you . . .'

'Exactly. Don't you let him. You do what I tell you. You tackle that steward. You'll make him jump, I bet,' insisted Captain Giles, waving his smouldering pipe impressively at me. Then he took three rapid puffs at it.

His aspect of triumphant acuteness was indescribable. Yet the man remained a strangely sympathetic creature. Benevolence radiated from him ridiculously, mildly, impressively. It was irritating too. But I pointed out coldly, as one who deals with the incomprehensible, that I didn't see any reason to expose myself to a snub from the fellow. He was a very unsatisfactory steward, and a miserable wretch besides, but I would just as soon think of tweaking his nose.

'Tweaking his nose,' said Captain Giles, in a scandalised tone. 'Much use it would be to you.'

That remark was so irrelevant that one could make no answer to it. But the sense of the absurdity was beginning at last to exercise its well-known fascination. I felt I must not let the man talk to me any more. I got up, observing curtly that he was too much for me – that I couldn't make him out.

Before I had time to move away he spoke again in a changed tone of obstinacy and puffing nervously at his pipe.

'Well – he's a – no account cuss – anyhow. You just – ask him. That's all.'

That new manner impressed me – or rather made me pause. But sanity asserting its sway, at once I left the verandah after giving him a mirthless smile. In a few strides I found myself in the dining-room, now cleared and empty. But during that short time various thoughts occurred to me, such as: that Giles had been making fun of me, expecting some amusement at my expense; that I probably looked silly and gullible; that I knew very little of life . . .

The door facing me across the dining-room flew open, to my extreme surprise. It was the door inscribed with the word 'Steward,' and the man himself ran out of his stuffy Philistinish lair in his absurd, hunted-animal manner, making for the garden door.

To this day I don't know what made me call after him, 'I say! Wait a minute.' Perhaps it was the sidelong glance he gave me; or possibly I was yet under the influence of Captain Giles's mysterious earnestness. Well, it was an impulse of some sort; an effect of that force somewhere within our lives which shapes them this way or that. For if these words had not escaped from my lips (my will had nothing to do with that) my existence would, to be sure, have been still a seaman's existence, but directed on now to me utterly inconceivable lines.

No. My will had nothing to do with it. Indeed, no sooner had I made that fateful noise than I became extremely sorry for it. Had the man stopped and faced me I would have had to retire in disorder. For I had no notion to carry out Captain Giles's idiotic joke, either at my own expense or at the expense of the steward.

But here the old human instinct of the chase came into play. He pretended to be deaf, and I, without thinking a second about it, dashed along my own side of the dining-table and cut him off at the very door.

'Why can't you answer when you are spoken to?' I asked roughly.

He leaned against the side of the door. He looked extremely wretched. Human nature is, I fear, not very nice right through. There are ugly spots in it. I found myself growing angry, and that, I believe, only because my quarry looked so woebegone. Miserable beggar!

I went for him without more ado. 'I understand there was an official communication to the Home from the Harbour Office this morning. Is that so?'

Instead of telling me to mind my own business, as he might have done, he began to whine with an undertone of impudence. He couldn't see me anywhere this morning. He couldn't be expected to run all over the town after me.

'Who wants you to?' I cried. And then my eyes became opened

to the inwardness of things and speeches, the triviality of which had been so baffling and tiresome.

I told him I wanted to know what was in that letter. My sternness of tone and behaviour was only half assumed. Curiosity can be a very fierce sentiment – at times.

He took refuge in a silly, muttering sulkiness. It was nothing to me, he mumbled. I had told him I was going home. And since I was going home he didn't see why he should . . .

That was the line of his argument, and it was irrelevant enough to be almost insulting. Insulting to one's intelligence, I mean.

In that twilight region between youth and maturity, in which I had my being then, one is peculiarly sensitive to that kind of insult. I am afraid my behaviour to the steward became very rough indeed. But it wasn't in him to face out anything or anybody. Drug habit or solitary tippling, perhaps. And when I forgot myself so far as to swear at him he broke down and began to shriek.

I don't mean to say that he made a great outcry. It was a cynical shrieking confession, only faint – piteously faint. It wasn't very coherent either, but sufficiently so to strike me dumb at first. I turned my eyes from him in righteous indignation, and perceived Captain Giles in the verandah doorway surveying quietly the scene, his own handiwork, if I may express it in that way. His smouldering black pipe was very noticeable in his big, paternal fist. So, too, was the glitter of his heavy gold watch-chain across the breast of his white tunic. He exhaled an atmosphere of virtuous sagacity thick enough for any innocent soul to fly to confidently. I flew to him.

'You would never believe it,' I cried. 'It was a notification that a master is wanted for some ship. There's a command apparently going about, and this fellow puts the thing in his pocket.'

The steward screamed out in accents of loud despair, 'You will be the death of me!'

The mighty slap he gave his wretched forehead was very loud, too. But when I turned to look at him he was no longer there. He had rushed away somewhere out of sight. This sudden disappearance made me laugh.

This was the end of the incident – for me. Captain Giles, however, staring at the place where the steward had been, began to haul at his gorgeous gold chain, till at last the watch came up from the deep pocket like solid truth from a well. Solemnly he lowered it down again, and only then said:

'Just three o'clock. You will be in time – if you don't lose any, that is.'

'In time for what?' I asked.

'Good Lord! For the Harbour Office. This must be looked into.'

Strictly speaking, he was right. But I've never had much taste for investigation, for showing people up and all that, no doubt, ethically meritorious kind of work. And my view of the episode was purely ethical. If any one had to be the death of the steward I didn't see why it shouldn't be Captain Giles himself, a man of age and standing, and a permanent resident. Whereas I, in comparison, felt myself a mere bird of passage in that port. In fact, it might have been said that I had already broken off my connection. I muttered that I didn't think – it was nothing to me ...

'Nothing?' repeated Captain Giles, giving some signs of quiet, deliberate indignation. 'Kent warned me you were a peculiar young fellow. You will tell me next that a command is nothing to you – and after all the trouble I've taken, too!'

'The trouble!' I murmured, uncomprehending. What trouble? All I could remember was being mystified and bored by his conversation for a solid hour at tiffin. And he called that taking a lot of trouble.

He was looking at me with a self-complacency which would have been odious in any other man. All at once, as if a page of a book had been turned over disclosing a word which made plain all that had gone before, I perceived that this matter had also another than an ethical aspect.

And still I did not move. Captain Giles lost his patience a little. With an angry puff at his pipe he turned his back on my hesitation.

But it was not hesitation on my part. I had been, if I may express myself so, put out of gear mentally. But as soon as I had convinced myself that this stale, unprofitable world of my discontent contained such a thing as a command to be seized, I recovered my powers of locomotion.

It's a good step from the Officers' Home to the Harbour Office; but with the magic word 'Command' in my head I found myself suddenly on the quay as if transported there in the twinkling of an eye, before a portal of dressed white stone above a flight of shallow white steps.

All this seemed to glide towards me swiftly. The whole great roadstead to the right was just a mere flicker of blue, and the dim cool hall swallowed me up out of the heat and glare of which I had not been aware till the very moment I passed in from it.

The broad inner staircase insinuated itself under my feet somehow. Command is a strong magic. The first human beings I perceived distinctly since I had parted with the indignant back of Captain Giles were the crew of the harbour steam-launch lounging on the spacious landing about the curtained archway of the shipping office.

It was there that my buoyancy abandoned me. The atmosphere of officialdom would kill anything that breathes the air of human endeavour, would extinguish hope and fear alike in the supremacy of paper and ink. I passed heavily under the curtain which the Malay coxwain[26] of the harbour launch raised for me. There was nobody in the office except the clerks, writing in two industrious rows. But the head shipping-master[27] hopped down from his elevation and hurried along on the thick mats to meet me in the broad central passage.

He had a Scottish name, but his complexion was of a rich olive hue, his short beard was jet black, and his eyes, also black, had a languishing expression. He asked confidentially:

'You want to see Him?'

All lightness of spirit and body having departed from me at the touch of officialdom, I looked at the scribe without animation, and asked in my turn wearily:

'What do you think? Is it any use?'

'My goodness! He has asked for you twice to-day.'

This emphatic He was the supreme authority, the Marine Superintendent, the Harbour-Master – a very great person in the eyes of every single quill-driver in the room. But that was nothing to the opinion he had of his own greatness.

Captain Ellis looked upon himself as a sort of divine (pagan) emanation, the deputy-Neptune for the circumambient seas. If he did not actually rule the waves, he pretended to rule the fate of the mortals whose lives were cast upon the waters.

This uplifting illusion made him inquisitorial and peremptory. And as his temperament was choleric there were fellows who were actually afraid of him. He was redoubtable, not in virtue of his office, but because of his unwarrantable assumptions. I had never had anything to do with him before.

I said, 'Oh! He has asked for me twice. Then, perhaps, I had better go in.'

'You must! You must!'

The shipping-master led the way with a mincing gait round the whole system of desks to a tall and important-looking door, which he opened with a deferential action of the arm.

He stepped right in (but without letting go of the handle) and, after gazing reverently down the room for a while, beckoned me in by a silent jerk of the head. Then he slipped out at once and shut the door after me most delicately.

Three lofty windows gave on the harbour. There was nothing in them but the dark-blue sparkling sea and the paler luminous blue of the sky. My eye caught in the depths and distances of these blue tones the white speck of some big ship just arrived and about to anchor in the outer roadstead. A ship from home – after perhaps ninety days at sea. There is something touching about a ship coming in from sea and folding her white wings for a rest.

The next thing I saw was the top-knot of silver hair surmounting Captain Ellis's smooth red face, which would have been apoplectic if it hadn't had such a fresh appearance.

Our deputy-Neptune had no beard on his chin, and there was no trident to be seen standing in a corner anywhere, like an umbrella. But his hand was holding a pen – the official pen, far mightier than the sword in making or marring the fortune of simple toiling men. He was looking over his shoulder at my advance.

When I had come well within range he saluted me by a nerve-shattering, 'Where have you been all this time?'

As it was no concern of his I did not take the slightest notice of the shot. I said simply that I had heard there was a master needed for some vessel, and being a sailing-ship man I thought I would apply . . .

He interrupted me. 'Why! Hang it! *You* are the right man for that job – if there had been twenty others after it. But no fear of that. They are all afraid to catch hold. That's what's the matter.'

He was irritated. I said innocently, 'Are they, sir? I wonder why?'

'Why!' he fumed. 'Afraid of the sails. Afraid of a white crew. Too much trouble. Too much work. Too long out here. Easy life and deck-chairs more their mark. Here I sit with the Consul-General's cable before me, and the only man fit for the job not to be found anywhere. I began to think you were funking it too . . .'

'I haven't been long getting to the office,' I remarked calmly.

'You have a good name out here, though,' he growled savagely, without looking at me.

'I am very glad to hear it from you, sir,' I said.

'Yes. But you are not on the spot when you are wanted. You know you weren't. That steward of yours wouldn't dare to neglect a message from this office. Where the devil did you hide yourself for the best part of the day?'

I only smiled kindly down on him, and he seemed to recollect himself, and asked me to take a seat. He explained that the master of a British ship having died in Bangkok the Consul-General had cabled to him a request for a competent man to be sent out to take command.

Apparently, in his mind, I was the man from the first, though for the looks of the thing the notification addressed to the Sailors' Home was general. An agreement had already been prepared. He gave it to me to read, and when I handed it back to him with the remark that I accepted its terms, the deputy-Neptune signed it, stamped it with his own exalted hand, folded it in four (it was a sheet of blue foolscap), and presented it to me – a gift of extraordinary potency, for, as I put it in my pocket, my head swam a little.

'This is your appointment to the command,' he said, with a certain gravity. 'An official appointment binding the owners to conditions which you have accepted. Now – when will you be ready to go?'

I said I would be ready that very day if necessary. He caught me at my word with great readiness. The steamer *Melita*[28] was leaving for Bangkok[29] that evening about seven. He would request her captain officially to give me a passage and wait for me till ten o'clock.

Then he rose from his office-chair, and I got up too. My head swam, there was no doubt about it, and I felt a heaviness of limbs as if they had grown bigger since I had sat down on that chair. I made my bow.

A subtle change in Captain Ellis's manner became perceptible as though he had laid aside the trident of deputy-Neptune. In reality, it was only his official pen that he had dropped on getting up.

CHAPTER TWO

He shook hands with me: 'Well, there you are, on your own appointed officially under my responsibility.'

He was actually walking with me to the door. What a distance off it seemed! I moved like a man in bonds. But we reached it at last. I opened it with the sensation of dealing with mere dream-stuff, and then at the last moment the fellowship of seamen asserted itself, stronger than the difference of age and station. It asserted itself in Captain Ellis's voice.

'Good-bye – and good luck to you,' he said so heartily that I could only give him a grateful glance. Then I turned and went out, never to see him again in my life. I had not made three steps into the outer office when I heard behind my back a gruff, loud, authoritative voice, the voice of our deputy-Neptune.

It was addressing the head shipping-master, who, having let me in, had, apparently, remained hovering in the middle distance ever since.

'Mr R., let the harbour launch have steam up to take the Captain here on board the *Melita* at half-past nine to-night.'

I was amazed at the startled assent of R.'s 'Yes, sir.' He ran before me out on the landing. My new dignity sat yet so lightly on me that I was not aware that it was I, the Captain, the object of this last graciousness. It seemed as if all of a sudden a pair of wings had grown on my shoulders. I merely skimmed along the polished floor.

But R. was impressed.

'I say!' he exclaimed on the landing, while the Malay crew of the steam-launch standing by looked stonily at the man for whom they were going to be kept on duty so late, away from their gambling, from their girls, or their pure domestic joys. 'I say! His own launch. What have you done to him?'

His stare was full of respectful curiosity. I was quite confounded.

'Was it for me? I hadn't the slightest notion,' I stammered out.

He nodded many times. 'Yes. And the last person who had it before you was a duke. So, there!'

I think he expected me to faint on the spot. But I was in too much of a hurry for emotional displays. My feelings were already in such a whirl that this staggering information did not seem to make the slightest difference. It fell into the seething cauldron of my brain, and I carried it off with me after a short but effusive passage of leave-taking with R.

The favour of the great throws an aureole round the fortunate object of its selection. That excellent man inquired whether he could do anything for me. He had known me only by sight, and he was well aware he would never see me again; I was, in common with the other seamen of the port, merely a subject for official writing, filling up of forms with all the artificial superiority of a man of pen and ink to the men who grapple with realities outside the consecrated walls of official buildings. What ghosts we must have been to him! Mere symbols to juggle with in books and heavy registers, without brains and muscles and perplexities; something hardly useful and decidedly inferior.

And he – the office hours being over – wanted to know if he could be of any use to me!

I ought, properly speaking – I ought to have been moved to tears. But I did not even think of it. It was only another miraculous manifestation of that day of miracles. I parted from him as if he had been a mere symbol. I floated down the staircase. I floated out of the official and imposing portal. I went on floating along.

I use that word rather than the word 'flew,' because I have a distinct impression that, though uplifted by my aroused youth, my movements were deliberate enough. To that mixed white, brown, and yellow portion of mankind, out abroad on their own affairs, I presented the appearance of a man walking rather sedately. And nothing in the way of abstraction could have equalled my deep detachment from the forms and colours of this world. It was, as it were, absolute.

And yet, suddenly, I recognised Hamilton. I recognised him without effort, without a shock, without a start. There he was, strolling towards the Harbour Office with his stiff, arrogant dignity. His red face made him noticeable at a distance. It flamed, over there, on the shady side of the street.

He had perceived me too. Something (unconscious exuberance of spirits, perhaps) moved me to wave my hand to him elaborately. This lapse from good taste happened before I was aware that I was capable of it.

The impact of my impudence stopped him short, much as a bullet might have done. I verily believe he staggered, though as far as I could see he didn't actually fall. I had gone past in a moment and did not turn my head. I had forgotten his existence.

The next ten minutes might have been ten seconds or ten centuries for all my consciousness had to do with it. People might have been falling dead around me, houses crumbling, guns firing, I wouldn't have known. I was thinking: 'By Jove! I have got it.' *It* being the command. It had come about in a way utterly unforeseen in my modest daydreams.

I perceived that my imagination had been running in conventional channels, and that my hopes had always been drab stuff. I had envisaged a command as a result of a slow course of promotion in the employ of some highly respectable firm. The reward of faithful service. Well, faithful service was all right. One would naturally give that for one's own sake, for the sake of the ship, for the love of the life of one's choice; not for the sake of the reward.

There is something distasteful in the notion of a reward.

And now, here, I had my command, absolutely in my pocket, in a way undeniable indeed, but most unexpected; beyond my imaginings, outside all reasonable expectations, and even notwithstanding the existence of some sort of obscure intrigue to keep it away from me. It is true that the intrigue was feeble, but it helped the feeling of wonder – as if I had been specially destined for that ship I did not know, by some power higher than the prosaic agencies of the commercial world.

A strange sense of exultation began to creep into me. If I had worked for that command ten years or more there would have been nothing of the kind. I was a little frightened.

'Let us be calm,' I said to myself.

Outside the door of the Officers' Home the wretched steward seemed to be waiting for me. There was a broad flight of a few steps, and he ran to and fro on the top of it as if chained there. A distressed cur. He looked as though his throat were too dry for him to bark.

I regret to say I stopped before going in. There had been a revolution in my moral nature. He waited open-mouthed, breathless, while I looked at him for half a minute.

'And you thought you could keep me out of it,' I said scathingly.

'You said you were going home,' he squeaked miserably. 'You said so. You said so.'

'I wonder what Captain Ellis will have to say to that excuse,' I uttered slowly, with a sinister meaning.

His lower jaw had been trembling all the time, and his voice was like the bleating of a sick goat. 'You have given me away. You have done for me.'

Neither his distress nor yet the sheer absurdity of it was able to disarm me. It was the first instance of harm being attempted to be done to me – at any rate, the first I had ever found out. And I was still young enough, still too much on this side of the shadow-line, not to be surprised and indignant at such things.

I gazed at him inflexibly. Let the beggar suffer. He slapped his forehead and I passed in, pursued, into the dining-room, by his screech, 'I always said you'd be the death of me.'

This clamour not only overtook me, but went ahead, as it were, on to the verandah and brought out Captain Giles.

He stood before me in the doorway in all the commonplace solidity of his wisdom. The gold chain glittered on his breast. He clutched a smouldering pipe.

I extended my hand to him warmly and he seemed surprised, but did respond heartily enough in the end, with a faint smile of superior knowledge which cut my thanks short as if with a knife. I don't think that more than one word came out. And even for that one, judging by the temperature of my face, I had blushed as if for a bad action. Assuming a detached tone, I wondered how on earth he had managed to spot the little underhand game that had been going on.

He murmured complacently that there were but few things done in the town that he could not see the inside of. And as to this house, he had been using it off and on for nearly ten years. Nothing that went on in it could escape his great experience. It had been no trouble to him. No trouble at all.

Then in his quiet, thick tone he wanted to know if I had complained formally of the steward's action.

I said that I hadn't – though, indeed, it was not for want of opportunity. Captain Ellis had gone for me bald-headed in a most ridiculous fashion for being out of the way when wanted.

'Funny old gentleman,' interjected Captain Giles. 'What did you say to that?'

'I said simply that I came along the very moment I heard of his message. Nothing more. I didn't want to hurt the steward. I would scorn to harm such an object. No. I made no complaint, but I believe he thinks I've done so. Let him think. He's got a fright that he won't forget in a hurry, for Captain Ellis would kick him out into the middle of Asia . . .'

'Wait a moment,' said Captain Giles, leaving me suddenly. I sat down feeling very tired, mostly in my head. Before I could start a train of thought he stood again before me, murmuring the excuse that he had to go and put the fellow's mind at ease.

I looked up with surprise. But in reality I was indifferent. He explained that he had found the steward lying face downwards on the horsehair sofa. He was all right now.

'He would not have died of fright,' I said contemptuously.

'No. But he might have taken an overdose out of one of those little bottles he keeps in his room,' Captain Giles argued seriously. 'The confounded fool has tried to poison himself once – a couple of years ago.'

'Really,' I said, without emotion. 'He doesn't seem very fit to live anyhow.'

'As to that, it may be said of a good many.'

'Don't exaggerate like this!' I protested, laughing irritably. 'But I wonder what this part of the world would do if you were to leave off looking after it, Captain Giles? Here you have got me a command and saved the steward's life in one afternoon. Though why you should have taken all that interest in either of us is more than I can understand.'

Captain Giles remained silent for a minute. Then gravely:

'He's not a bad steward really. He can find a good cook, at any rate. And, what's more, he can keep him when found. I remember the cooks we had here before his time . . .'

I must have made a movement of impatience, because he interrupted himself with an apology for keeping me yarning there, while no doubt I needed all my time to get ready.

What I really needed was to be alone for a bit. I seized this opening hastily. My bedroom was a quiet refuge in an apparently uninhabited wing of the building. Having absolutely nothing to do (for I had not unpacked my things), I sat down on the bed and abandoned myself to the influences of the hour. To the unexpected influences . . .

And first I wondered at my state of mind. Why was I not more surprised? Why? Here I was, invested with a command in the twinkling of an eye, not in the common course of human affairs, but more as if by enchantment. I ought to have been lost in astonishment. But I wasn't. I was very much like people in fairy tales. Nothing ever astonishes them. When a fully appointed gala coach is produced out of a pumpkin to take her to a ball Cinderella does not exclaim. She gets in quietly and drives away to her high fortune.

Captain Ellis (a fierce sort of fairy) had produced a command out of a drawer almost as unexpectedly as in a fairy tale. But a command is an abstract idea, and it seemed a sort of 'lesser marvel' till it flashed upon me that it involved the concrete existence of a ship.

A ship! My ship! She was mine, more absolutely mine for possession and care than anything in the world; an object of responsibility and devotion. She was there waiting for me, spellbound, unable to move, to live, to get out into the world (till I came), like an enchanted princess. Her call had come to me as if from the clouds. I had never suspected her existence. I didn't know how she looked, I had barely heard her name, and yet we were indissolubly united for a certain portion of our future, to sink or swim together!

A sudden passion of anxious impatience rushed through my veins, and gave me such a sense of the intensity of existence as I have never felt before or since. I discovered how much of a seaman I was, in heart, in mind, and, as it were, physically – a man exclusively of sea and ships; the sea the only world that counted, and the ships the test of manliness, of temperament, of courage and fidelity – and of love.

I had an exquisite moment. It was unique also. Jumping up from my seat, I paced up and down my room for a long time. But when I came into the dining-room I behaved with sufficient composure. Only I couldn't eat anything at dinner.

Having declared my intention not to drive but to walk down to the quay, I must render the wretched steward justice that he bestirred himself to find me some coolies [1] for the luggage. They departed, carrying all my worldly possessions (except a little money I had in my pocket) slung from a long pole. Captain Giles volunteered to walk down with me.

We followed the sombre, shaded alley across the Esplanade. It was moderately cool there under the trees. Captain Giles remarked, with a sudden laugh, 'I know who's jolly thankful at having seen the last of you.'

I guessed that he meant the steward. The fellow had borne himself to me in a sulkily frightened manner at the last. I expressed my wonder that he should have tried to do me a bad turn for no reason at all.

'Don't you see that what he wanted was to get rid of our friend Hamilton by dodging him in front of you for that job? That would have removed him for good, see?'

'Heavens!' I exclaimed, feeling humiliated somehow. 'Can it be possible? What a fool he must be! That overbearing, impudent loafer! Why! He couldn't . . . And yet he's nearly done it, I believe; for the Harbour Office was bound to send somebody.'

'Aye. A fool like our steward can be dangerous sometimes,' declared Captain Giles sententiously. 'Just because he is a fool,' he added, imparting further instruction in his complacent, low tones. 'For,' he continued in the manner of a set demonstration, 'no sensible person would risk being kicked out of the only berth between himself and starvation just to get rid of a simple annoyance – a small worry. Would he now?'

'Well, no,' I conceded, restraining a desire to laugh at that something mysteriously earnest in delivering the conclusions of his wisdom as though they were the product of prohibited operations. 'But that fellow looks as if he were rather crazy. He must be.'

'As to that, I believe everybody in the world is a little mad,' he announced quietly.

'You make no exceptions?' I inquired, just to hear his answer.

He kept silent for a little while, then got home in an effective manner:

'Why! Kent says that even of you.'

'Does he?' I retorted, extremely embittered all at once against my former captain. 'There's nothing of that in the written character from him which I've got in my pocket. Has he given you any instances of my lunacy?'

Captain Giles explained in a conciliating tone that it had been only a friendly remark in reference to my abrupt leaving the ship for no apparent reason.

I muttered grumpily, 'Oh! leaving his ship,' and mended my pace. He kept up by my side in the deep gloom of the avenue as if it were his conscientious duty to see me out of the colony as an undesirable character. He panted a little, which was rather pathetic in a way. But I was not moved. On the contrary. His discomfort gave me a sort of malicious pleasure.

Presently I relented, slowed down, and said:

'What I really wanted was to get a fresh grip. I felt it was time. Is that so very mad?'

He made no answer. We were issuing from the avenue. On the bridge over the canal a dark, irresolute figure seemed to be awaiting something or somebody.

It was a Malay policeman, barefooted, in his blue uniform. The silver band on his little round cap shone dimly in the light of the street lamp. He peered in our direction timidly.

Before we could come up to him he turned about and walked in front of us in the direction of the jetty. The distance was some hundred yards; and then I found my coolies squatting on their heels. They had kept the pole on their shoulders, and all my worldly goods, still tied to the pole, were resting on the ground between them. As far as the eye could reach along the quay there was not another soul abroad except the police peon, who saluted us.

It seems he had detained the coolies as suspicious characters, and had forbidden them the jetty. But at a sign from me he took off the embargo with alacrity. The two patient fellows, rising together with a faint grunt, trotted off along the planks, and I prepared to take my leave of Captain Giles, who stood there with an air as though his mission was drawing to a close. It could not be denied that he had done it all. And while I hesitated about an appropriate sentence he made himself heard:

'I expect you'll have your hands pretty full of tangled-up business.'

I asked him what made him think so; and he answered that it was his general experience of the world. Ship a long time away from her port, owners inaccessible by cable, and the only man who could explain matters dead and buried.

'And you yourself new to the business in a way,' he concluded, in a sort of unanswerable tone.

'Don't insist,' I said. 'I know it only too well. I only wish you could impart to me some small portion of your experience before I go. As it can't be done in ten minutes I had better not begin to ask you. There's that harbour launch waiting for me too. But I won't feel really at peace till I have that ship of mine out in the Indian Ocean.'

He remarked casually that from Bangkok to the Indian Ocean was a pretty long step. And this murmur, like a dim flash from a dark lantern, showed me for a moment the broad belt of islands and reefs between that unknown ship, which was mine, and the freedom of the great waters of the globe.

But I felt no apprehension. I was familiar enough with the Archipelago by that time. Extreme patience and extreme care would see me through the region of broken land, of faint airs, and of dead water to where I would feel at last my command swing on the great swell and list over to the great breath of regular winds, that would give her the feeling of a large, more intense life. The road would be long. All roads are long that lead towards one's heart's desire. But this road my mind's eye could see on a chart, professionally, with all its complications and difficulties, yet simple enough in a way. One is a seaman, or one is not. And I had no doubt of being one.

The only part I was a stranger to was the Gulf of Siam. And I mentioned this to Captain Giles. Not that I was concerned very much. It belonged to the same region the nature of which I knew, into whose very soul I seemed to have looked during the last months of that existence with which I had broken now, suddenly, as one parts with some enchanting company.

'The gulf . . . Aye! A funny piece of water – that,' said Captain Giles.

Funny, in this connection, was a vague word. The whole thing sounded like an opinion uttered by a cautious person mindful of actions for slander.

I didn't inquire as to the nature of that funniness. There was really no time. But at the very last he volunteered a warning.

'Whatever you do, keep to the east side of it. The west side is dangerous at this time of the year. Don't let anything tempt you over. You'll find nothing but trouble there.'

Though I could hardly imagine what could tempt me to involve my ship amongst the currents and reefs of the Malay shore, I thanked him for the advice.

He gripped my extended arm warmly, and the end of our acquaintance came suddenly in the words, 'Good-night.'

That was all he said: 'Good-night.' Nothing more. I don't know what I intended to say, but surprise made me swallow it, whatever it was. I choked slightly, and then exclaimed, with a sort of nervous haste, 'Oh! Good-night, Captain Giles, good-night.'

His movements were always deliberate, but his back had receded some distance along the deserted quay before I collected myself enough to follow his example and made a half-turn in the direction of the jetty.

Only my movements were not deliberate. I hurried down to the steps and leaped into the launch. Before I had fairly landed in her stern-sheets [2] the slim little craft darted away from the jetty with a sudden swirl of her propeller and the hard rapid puffing of the exhaust in her vaguely gleaming brass funnel amidships.

The misty churning at her stern was the only sound in the world. The shore lay plunged in the silence of the deepest slumber. I watched the town recede still and soundless in the hot night till the abrupt hail, 'Steam-launch, ahoy!' made me spin round face forward. We were close to a white, ghostly steamer. Lights shone on her decks, in her port-holes. And the same voice shouted from her, 'Is that our passenger?'

'It is,' I yelled.

Her crew had been obviously on the jump. I could hear them running about. The modern spirit of haste was loudly vocal in the orders to 'Heave away on the cable' – to 'Lower the side-ladder,' and in urgent requests to me to 'Come along, sir! We have been delayed three hours for you . . . Our time is seven o'clock, you know!'

I stepped on the deck. I said, 'No! I don't know.' The spirit of modern hurry was embodied in a thin, long-armed, long-legged man, with a closely clipped grey beard. His meagre hand was hot and dry. He declared feverishly:

'I am hanged if I would have waited another five minutes – harbour-master or no harbour-master.'

'That's your own business,' I said. 'I didn't ask you to wait for me.'

'I hope you don't expect any supper,' he burst out. 'This isn't a boarding-house afloat. You are the first passenger I ever had in my life, and I hope to goodness you will be the last.'

I made no answer to this hospitable communication; and, indeed, he didn't wait for any, bolting away on to his bridge to get his ship under way.

For the four days he had me on board he did not depart from that half-hostile attitude. His ship having been delayed three hours on my account, he couldn't forgive me for not being a more distinguished person. He was not exactly outspoken about it, but that feeling of annoyed wonder was peeping out perpetually in his talk.

He was absurd.

He was also a man of much experience, which he liked to trot out; but no greater contrast with Captain Giles could have been imagined. He would have amused me if I had wanted to be amused. But I did not want to be amused. I was like a lover looking forward to a meeting. Human hostility was nothing to me. I thought of my unknown ship. It was amusement enough, torment enough, occupation enough.

He perceived my state, for his wits were sufficiently sharp for that, and he poked sly fun at my preoccupation in the manner some nasty, cynical old men assume towards the dreams and illusions of youth. I, on my side, refrained from questioning him as to the appearance of my ship, though I knew that being in Bangkok every month or so he must have known her by sight. I was not going to expose the ship, my ship! to some slighting reference.

He was the first really unsympathetic man I had ever come in contact with. My education was far from being finished, though I didn't know it. No! I didn't know it.

All I knew was that he disliked me, and had some contempt for my person. Why? Apparently because his ship had been delayed three hours on my account. Who was I to have such a thing done for me? Such a thing had never been done for him. It was a sort of jealous indignation.

My expectation, mingled with fear, was wrought to its highest pitch. How slow had been the days of the passage, and how soon they were over. One morning, early, we crossed the bar,[3] and while the sun was rising splendidly over the flat spaces of the land we steamed up the innumerable bends,[4] passed under the shadow of the great gilt pagoda,[5] and reached the outskirts of the town.

There it was, spread largely on both banks, the Oriental capital which had as yet suffered no white conqueror; an expanse of brown houses of bamboo, of mats, of leaves, of a vegetable-matter style of architecture, sprung out of the brown soil on the banks of the muddy river. It was amazing to think that in those miles of human habitations there was not probably half a dozen pounds of nails. Some of those houses of sticks and grass, like the nests of an aquatic race, clung to the low shores. Others seemed to grow out of the water; others again floated in long anchored rows in the very middle of the stream. Here and there in the distance, above the crowded mob of low, brown roof ridges, towered great piles of masonry, King's Palace,[6] temples, gorgeous and dilapidated, crumbling under the vertical sunlight, tremendous, overpowering, almost palpable, which seemed to enter one's breast with the breath of one's nostrils, and soak into one's limbs through every pore of one's skin.

The ridiculous victim of jealousy had for some reason or other to stop his engines just then. The steamer drifted slowly up with the tide. Oblivious of my new surroundings I walked the deck, in anxious, deadened abstraction, a commingling of romantic reverie with a very practical survey of my qualifications. For the time was approaching for me to behold my command, and to prove my worth in the ultimate test of my profession.

Suddenly I heard myself called by that imbecile. He was beckoning me to come up on his bridge.

I didn't care very much for that, but, as it seemed that he had something particular to say, I went up the ladder.

He laid his hand on my shoulder and gave me a slight turn, pointing with his other arm at the same time.

'There! That's your ship, Captain,' he said.

I felt a thump in my breast – only one, as if my heart had then ceased to beat. There were ten or more ships moored along the bank, and the one he meant was partly hidden from my sight by her next astern. He said, 'We'll drift abreast her in a moment.'

What was his tone? Mocking? Threatening? Or only indifferent? I could not tell. I suspected some malice in this unexpected manifestation of interest.

He left me, and I leaned over the rail of the bridge looking over the side. I dared not raise my eyes. Yet it had to be done – and, indeed, I could not have helped myself. I believe I trembled.

But directly my eyes had rested on my ship all my fear vanished. It went off swiftly, like a bad dream. Only that a dream leaves no shame behind it, and that I felt a momentary shame at my unworthy suspicions.

Yes, there she was.[7] Her hull, her rigging filled my eye with a great content. That feeling of life-emptiness which had made me so restless for the last few months lost its bitter plausibility, its evil influence, dissolved in a flow of joyous emotion.

At the first glance I saw that she was a high-class vessel, a harmonious creature in the lines of her fine body, in the proportioned tallness of her spars. Whatever her age and her history, she had preserved the stamp of her origin. She was one of those craft that, in virtue of their design and complete finish, will never look old. Amongst her companions moored to the bank, and all bigger than herself, she looked like a creature of high breed – an Arab steed in a string of cart-horses.

A voice behind me said in a nasty equivocal tone, 'I hope you are satisfied with her, Captain.' I did not even turn my head. It was the master of the steamer, and whatever he meant, whatever he thought of her, I knew that, like some rare women, she was one of those creatures whose mere existence is enough to awaken an unselfish delight. One feels that it is good to be in the world in which she has her being.

That illusion of life and character which charms one in men's finest handiwork radiated from her. An enormous balk [8] of teakwood timber swung over her hatchway; lifeless matter, looking heavier and bigger than anything aboard of her. When they started lowering it the surge of the tackle sent a quiver through her from water-line to the trucks [9] up the fine nerves of her rigging, as though she had shuddered at the weight. It seemed cruel to load her so . . .

Half an hour later, putting my foot on her deck for the first time, I received the feeling of deep physical satisfaction. Nothing could equal the fullness of that moment, the ideal completeness of that emotional experience which had come to me without the preliminary toil and disenchantments of an obscure career.

My rapid glance ran over her, enveloped, appropriated the form concreting the abstract sentiment of my command. A lot of details perceptible to a seaman struck my eye vividly in that instant. For the rest, I saw her disengaged from the material conditions of her being. The shore to which she was moored was as if it did not exist. What were to me all the countries of the globe? In all the parts of the world washed by navigable waters our relation to each other would be the same – and more intimate than there are words to express in the language. Apart from that, every scene and episode would be a mere passing show. The very gang of yellow coolies busy about the main hatch was less substantial than the stuff dreams are made of. For who on earth would dream of Chinamen? . . .

I went aft, ascended the poop, where, under the awning, gleamed the brasses of the yacht-like fittings, the polished surfaces of the rails, the glass of the skylights. Right aft two seamen, busy cleaning the steering gear, with the reflected ripples of light running playfully up their bent backs, went on with their work, unaware of me and of the almost affectionate glance I threw at them in passing towards the companion-way [10] of the cabin.

The doors stood wide open, the slide was pushed right back. The half-turn of the staircase cut off the view of the lobby.[11] A low humming ascended from below, but it stopped abruptly at the sound of my descending footsteps.

CHAPTER THREE

The first thing I saw down there was the upper part of a man's body projecting backwards, as it were, from one of the doors at the foot of the stairs. His eyes looked at me very wide and still. In one hand he held a dinner plate, in the other a cloth.

'I am your new captain,' I said quietly.

In a moment, in the twinkling of an eye, he had got rid of the plate and the cloth and jumped to open the cabin door. As soon as I passed into the saloon he vanished, but only to reappear instantly, buttoning up a jacket he had put on with the swiftness of a 'quick-change' artist.

'Where's the chief mate?' I asked.

'In the hold, I think, sir. I saw him go down the after-hatch ten minutes ago.'

'Tell him I am on board.'

The mahogany table under the skylight shone in the twilight like a dark pool of water. The sideboard, surmounted by a wide looking-glass in an ormolu [1] frame, had a marble top. It bore a pair of silver-plated lamps and some other pieces – obviously a harbour display. The saloon itself was panelled in two kinds of wood in the excellent, simple taste prevailing when the ship was built

I sat down in the arm-chair at the head of the table – the captain's chair, with a small tell-tale compass swung above it – a mute reminder of unremitting vigilance.

A succession of men had sat in that chair. I became aware of that thought suddenly, vividly, as though each had left a little of himself between the four walls of these ornate bulkheads; [2] as if a sort of composite soul, the soul of command, had whispered suddenly to mine of long days at sea and of anxious moments.

'You, too!' it seemed to say, 'you, too, shall taste of that peace and that unrest in a searching intimacy with your own self – obscure as we were, and as supreme in the face of all the winds and all the seas, in an immensity that receives no impress, preserves no memories, and keeps no reckoning of lives.'

Deep within the tarnished ormolu frame, in the hot half-light sifted through the awning, I saw my own face propped between my hands. And I stared back at myself with the perfect detachment of distance, rather with curiosity than with any other feeling, except of some sympathy for this latest representative of what for all intents and purposes was a dynasty; continuous not in blood, indeed, but in its experience, in its training, in its conception of duty, and in the blessed simplicity of its traditional point of view on life.

It struck me that this quietly staring man, whom I was watching, both as if he were myself and somebody else, was not exactly a lonely figure. He had his place in a line of men whom he did not know, of whom he had never heard; but who were fashioned by the same influences, whose souls in relation to their humble life's work had no secrets for him.

Suddenly I perceived that there was another man in the saloon, standing a little on one side and looking intently at me. The chief mate. His long, red moustache determined the character of his physiognomy, which struck me as pugnacious in (strange to say) a ghastly sort of way.

How long had he been there looking at me, appraising me in my unguarded, daydreaming state? I would have been more disconcerted if, having the clock set in the top of the mirror-frame right in front of me, I had not noticed that its long hand had hardly moved at all.

I could not have been in the cabin more than two minutes altogether. Say three . . . So he could not have been watching me more than a mere fraction of a minute luckily. Still, I regretted the occurrence.

But I showed nothing of it as I rose leisurely (it had to be leisurely) and greeted him with perfect friendliness.

There was something reluctant, and at the same time attentive, in his bearing. His name was Burns.[3] We left the cabin and went round the ship together. His face in the full light of day appeared very worn, meagre, even haggard. Somehow I had a delicacy as to looking too often at him; his eyes, on the contrary, remained fairly glued on my face. They were greenish, and had an expectant expression.

He answered all my questions readily enough, but my ear seemed to catch a tone of unwillingness. The second officer, with three or four hands, was busy forward. The mate mentioned his name, and I nodded to him in passing. He was very young. He struck me as rather a cub.

When we returned below I sat down on one end of a deep, semicircular, or, rather, semioval settee, upholstered in red plush. It extended right across the whole after-end of the cabin. Mr Burns, motioned to sit down, dropped into one of the swivel-chairs round the table, and kept his eyes on me as persistently as ever, and with that strange air as if all this were make-believe, and he expected me to get up, burst into a laugh, slap him on the back, and vanish from the cabin.

There was an odd stress in the situation which began to make me uncomfortable. I tried to react against this vague feeling.

'It's only my inexperience,' I thought.

In the face of that man, several years, I judged, older than myself, I became aware of what I had left already behind me – my youth. And that was indeed poor comfort. Youth is a fine thing, a mighty power – as long as one does not think of it. I felt I was becoming self-conscious. Almost against my will I assumed a moody gravity. I said, 'I see you have kept her in very good order, Mr Burns.'

Directly I had uttered these words I asked myself angrily why the deuce did I want to say that? Mr Burns in answer had only blinked at me. What on earth did he mean?

I fell back on a question which had been in my thoughts for a long time – the most natural question on the lips of any seaman whatever joining a ship. I voiced it (confound this self-consciousness) in a *dégagé*⁴ cheerful tone, 'I suppose she can travel – what?'

Now a question like this might have been answered normally, either in accents of apologetic sorrow or with a visibly suppressed pride, in a 'I don't want to boast, but you shall see,' sort of tone. There are sailors, too, who would have been roughly outspoken: 'Lazy brute,' or openly delighted: 'She's a flyer.' Two ways, if four manners.

But Mr Burns found another way, a way of his own which had, at all events, the merit of saving his breath, if no other.

Again he did not say anything. He only frowned. And it was an angry frown. I waited. Nothing more came.

'What's the matter? . . . Can't you tell after being nearly two years in the ship?' I addressed him sharply.

He looked as startled for a moment as though he had discovered my presence only that very moment. But this passed off almost at once. He put on an air of indifference. But I suppose he thought it better to say something. He said that a ship needed, just like a man, the chance to show the best she could do, and that this ship had never had a chance since he had been on board of her. Not that he could remember. The last captain [5] . . . He paused.

'Has he been so very unlucky?' I asked, with frank incredulity. Mr Burns turned his eyes away from me. No, the late captain was not an unlucky man. One couldn't say that. But he had not seemed to want to make use of his luck.

Mr Burns – man of enigmatic moods – made this statement with an inanimate face, and staring wilfully at the rudder-casing.[6] The statement itself was obscurely suggestive. I asked quietly:

'Where did he die?'

'In this saloon. Just where you are sitting now,' answered Mr Burns.

I repressed a silly impulse to jump up; but upon the whole I was relieved to hear that he had not died in the bed which was now to be mine. I pointed out to the chief mate that what I really wanted to know was where he had buried his late captain.

Mr Burns said that it was at the entrance to the gulf. A roomy grave; a sufficient answer. But the mate, overcoming visibly something within him – something like a curious reluctance to believe in my advent (as an irrevocable fact, at any rate), did not stop at that – though, indeed, he may have wished to do so.

As a compromise with his feelings, I believe, he addressed himself persistently to the rudder-casing, so that to me he had the appearance of a man talking in solitude, a little unconsciously, however.

His tale was that at seven bells in the forenoon watch [7] he had all hands mustered on the quarter-deck, and told them that they had better go down to say good-bye to the captain.

Those words, as if grudged to an intruding personage, were enough for me to evoke vividly that strange ceremony: The bare-footed, bareheaded seamen crowding shyly into that cabin, a small mob pressed against that sideboard, uncomfortable rather than moved, shirts open on sunburnt chests, weather-beaten faces, and all staring at the dying man with the same grave and expectant expression.

'Was he conscious?' I asked.

'He didn't speak, but he moved his eyes to look at them,' said the mate.

After waiting a moment Mr Burns motioned the crew to leave the cabin, but he detained the two eldest men to stay with the captain while he went on deck with his sextant [8] to 'take the sun.' It was getting towards noon, and he was anxious to obtain a good observation for latitude. When he returned below to put his sextant away he found that the two men had retreated out into the lobby. Through the open door he had a view of the captain lying easy against the pillows. He had 'passed away' while Mr Burns was taking his observation. As near noon as possible. He had hardly changed his position.

Mr Burns sighed, glanced at me inquisitively, as much as to say, 'Aren't you going yet?' and then turned his thoughts from his new captain back to the old, who, being dead, had no authority, was not in anybody's way, and was much easier to deal with.

Mr Burns dealt with him at some length. He was a peculiar man – of sixty-five about – iron-grey, hard-faced, obstinate, and un-communicative. He used to keep the ship loafing at sea for in-scrutable reasons. Would come on deck at night sometimes, take some sail off her, God only knows why or wherefore, then go below, shut himself up in his cabin, and play on the violin for hours – till daybreak, perhaps. In fact, he spent most of his time day or night playing the violin. That was when the fit took him. Very loud, too.

It came to this, that Mr Burns mustered his courage one day and remonstrated earnestly with the captain. Neither he nor the second mate could get a wink of sleep in their watches below for the noise ... And how could they be expected to keep awake while on duty? he pleaded. The answer of that stern man was that if he and the second mate didn't like the noise, they were welcome to pack up their traps and walk over the side. When this alternative was offered the ship happened to be six hundred miles from the nearest land.

Mr Burns at this point looked at me with an air of curiosity. I began to think that my predecessor was a remarkably peculiar old man.

But I had to hear stranger things yet. It came out that this stern, grim, wind-tanned, rough, sea-salted, taciturn sailor of sixty-five was not only an artist, but a lover as well. In Haiphong,[9] when they got there after a course of most unprofitable peregrinations (during which the ship was nearly lost twice), he got himself, in Mr Burns's own words, 'mixed up' with some woman. Mr Burns had had no personal knowledge of that affair, but positive evidence of it existed in the shape of a photograph taken in Haiphong. Mr Burns found it in one of the drawers in the captain's room.

In due course I, too, saw that amazing human document (I even threw it overboard later). There he sat, with his hands reposing on his knees, bald, squat, grey, bristly, recalling a wild boar somehow; and by his side towered an awful, mature, white female with rapacious nostrils and a cheaply ill-omened stare in her enormous eyes. She was disguised in some semi-oriental, vulgar, fancy costume. She resembled a low-cast medium, or one of those women who tell fortunes by cards for half a crown. And yet she was striking. A professional sorceress from the slums. It was incomprehensible. There was something awful in the thought that she was the last reflection of the world of passion for the fierce soul which seemed to look at one out of the sardonically savage face of that old seaman. However, I noticed that she was holding some musical instrument – guitar or mandoline – in her hand. Perhaps that was the secret of her sortilege.

For Mr Burns that photograph explained why the unloaded ship was kept sweltering at anchor for three weeks in a pestilential hot harbour without air. They lay there and gasped. The captain, appearing now and then on short visits, mumbled to Mr Burns unlikely tales about some letters he was waiting for.

Suddenly, after vanishing for a week, he came on board in the middle of the night and took the ship out to sea with the first break of dawn. Daylight showed him looking wild and ill. The mere getting clear of the land took two days, and somehow or other they bumped slightly on a reef. However, no leak developed, and the captain, growling 'No matter,' informed Mr Burns that he had made up his mind to take the ship to Hong-Kong[10] and dry-dock her there.

At this Mr Burns was plunged into despair. For indeed, to beat up to Hong-Kong against a fierce monsoon, with a ship not sufficiently ballasted, and with her supply of water not completed, was an insane project.

But the captain growled peremptorily, 'Stick her at it,' and Mr Burns, dismayed and enraged, stuck her at it, and kept her at it, blowing away sails, straining the spars, exhausting the crew – nearly maddened by the absolute conviction that the attempt was impossible, and was bound to end in some catastrophe.

Meantime the captain, shut up in his cabin and wedged in a corner of his settee against the crazy bounding of the ship, played the violin – or, at any rate, made continuous noise on it.

When he appeared on deck he would not speak, and not always answer when spoken to. It was obvious that he was ill in some mysterious manner, and beginning to break up.

As the days went by, the sounds of the violin became less and less loud, till at last only a feeble scratching would meet Mr Burns's ear as he stood in the saloon listening outside the door of the captain's state-room.

One afternoon in perfect desperation he burst into that room, and made such a scene, tearing his hair and shouting such horrid imprecations, that he cowed the contemptuous spirit of the sick man. The water-tanks were low, they had not gained fifty miles in a fortnight. She would never reach Hong-Kong.

It was like fighting desperately towards destruction for the ship and the men. This was evident without argument. Mr Burns, losing all restraint, put his face close to his captain's and fairly yelled, 'You, sir, are going out of the world. But I can't wait till you are dead before I put the helm up.[11] You must do it yourself. You must do it now!'

The man on the couch snarled in contempt, 'So I am going out of the world – am I?'

'Yes, sir – you haven't many days left in it,' said Mr Burns, calming down. 'One can see it by your face.'

'My face, eh? . . . Well, put the helm up, and be damned to you.'

Burns flew on deck, got the ship before the wind, then came down again, composed but resolute.

'I've shaped a course for Pulo Condor,[12] sir,' he said. 'When we make it, if you are still with us, you'll tell me into what port you wish me to take the ship, and I'll do it.'

The old man gave him a look of savage spite, and said those atrocious words in deadly, slow tones:

'If I had my wish, neither the ship nor any of you would ever reach a port. And I hope you won't.'

Mr Burns was profoundly shocked. I believe he was positively frightened at the time. It seems, however, that he managed to produce such an effective laugh that it was the old man's turn to be frightened. He shrank within himself, and turned his back on him.

'And his head was not gone then,' Mr Burns assured me excitedly. 'He meant every word of it.'

Such was practically the late captain's last speech. No connected sentence passed his lips afterwards. That night he used the last of his strength to throw his fiddle over the side. No one had actually seen him in the act, but after his death Mr Burns couldn't find the thing anywhere. The empty case was very much in evidence, but the fiddle was clearly not in the ship. And where else could it have gone to but overboard?

'Threw his violin overboard!' I exclaimed.

'He did,' cried Mr Burns excitedly. 'And it's my belief he would have tried to take the ship down with him if it had been in human power. He never meant her to see home again. He wouldn't write to his owners, he never wrote to his old wife either – he wasn't going to. He had made up his mind to cut adrift from everything. That's what it was. He didn't care for business, or freights, or for making a passage – or anything. He meant to have gone wandering about the world till he lost her with all hands.'

Mr Burns looked like a man who had escaped great danger. For a little he would have exclaimed, 'If it hadn't been for me!' And the transparent innocence of his indignant eyes was underlined quaintly by the arrogant pair of moustaches which he proceeded to twist, and as if extend, horizontally.

I might have smiled if I had not been busy with my own sensations, which were not those of Mr Burns. I was already the man in command. My sensations could not be like those of any other man on board. In that community I stood, like a king in his country, in a class all by myself. I mean an hereditary king, not a mere elected head of a state. I was brought there to rule by an agency as remote from the people and as inscrutable almost to them as the Grace of God.

And like a member of a dynasty, feeling a semi-mystical bond with the dead, I was profoundly shocked by my immediate predecessor.

That man had been in all essentials but his age just such another man as myself. Yet the end of his life was a complete act of treason, the betrayal of a tradition which seemed to me as imperative as any guide on earth could be. It appeared that even at sea a man could become the victim of evil spirits. I felt on my face the breath of unknown powers that shape our destinies.

Not to let the silence last too long, I asked Mr Burns if he had written to his captain's wife. He shook his head. He had written to nobody.

In a moment he became sombre. He never thought of writing. It took him all his time to watch incessantly the loading of the ship by a rascally Chinese stevedore. In this Mr Burns gave me the first glimpse of the real chief mate's soul which dwelt uneasily in his body.

He mused, then hastened on with gloomy force.

'Yes! The captain died as near noon as possible. I looked through his papers in the afternoon. I read the service over him at sunset, and then I stuck the ship's head north and brought her in here. I – brought – her – in.'

He struck the table with his fist.

'She would hardly have come in by herself,' I observed. 'But why didn't you make for Singapore instead?'

His eyes wavered. 'The nearest port,' he muttered sullenly.

I had framed the question in perfect innocence, but this answer (the difference in distance was insignificant) and his manner offered me a clue to the simple truth. He took the ship to a port where he expected to be confirmed in his temporary command from lack of a qualified master to put over his head; whereas Singapore, he surmised justly, would be full of qualified men. But his naïve reasoning forgot to take into account the telegraph cable [13] reposing on the bottom of the very Gulf up which he had turned that ship which he imagined himself to have saved from destruction. Hence the bitter flavour of our interview. I tasted it more and more distinctly – and it was less and less to my taste.

'Look here, Mr Burns,' I began very firmly. 'You may as well understand that I did not run after this command. It was pushed in my way. I've accepted it. I am here to take the ship home first of all, and you may be sure that I shall see to it that every one of you on board here does his duty to that end. This is all I have to say – for the present.'

He was on his feet by this time, but instead of taking his dismissal he remained with trembling, indignant lips, and looking at me hard as though, really, after this, there was nothing for me to do in common decency but to vanish from his outraged sight. Like all very simple emotional states this was moving. I felt sorry for him – almost sympathetic, till (seeing that I did not vanish) he spoke in a tone of forced restraint:

'If I hadn't a wife and a child at home you may be sure, sir, I would have asked you to let me go the very minute you came on board.'

I answered him with a matter-of-course calmness as though some remote third person were in question.

'And I, Mr Burns, would not have let you go. You have signed the ship's articles as chief officer, and till they are terminated at the final port of discharge I shall expect you to attend to your duty, and give me the benefit of your experience to the best of your ability.'

Stony incredulity lingered in his eyes; but it broke down before my friendly attitude. With a slight upward toss of his arms (I got to know that gesture well afterwards) he bolted out of the cabin.

We might have saved ourselves that little passage of harmless sparring. Before many days had elapsed it was Mr Burns who was pleading with me anxiously not to leave him behind; while I could only return him but doubtful answers. The whole thing took on a somewhat tragic complexion.

And this horrible problem was only an extraneous episode, a mere complication in the general problem of how to get that ship – which was mine with her appurtenances and her men, with her body and her spirit now slumbering in that pestilential river – how to get her out to sea.

Mr Burns, while still acting captain, had hastened to sign a charter-party [14] which in an ideal world without guile would have been an excellent document. Directly I ran my eye over it I foresaw trouble ahead unless the people of the other part were quite exceptionally fair-minded and open to argument.

Mr Burns, to whom I imparted my fears, chose to take great umbrage at them. He looked at me with that usual incredulous stare, and said bitterly:

'I suppose, sir, you want to make out I've acted like a fool?'

I told him, with my systematic kindliness, which always seemed to augment his surprise, that I did not want to make out anything. I would leave that to the future.

And, sure enough, the future brought in a lot of trouble. There were days when I used to remember Captain Giles with nothing short of abhorrence. His confounded acuteness had let me in for this job; while his prophecy that I 'would have my hands full' coming true, made it appear as if done on purpose to play an evil joke on my young innocence.

Yes. I had my hands full of complications which were most valuable as 'experience.' People have a great opinion of the advantages of experience. But in that connection experience means always something disagreeable as opposed to the charm and innocence of illusions.

I must say I was losing mine rapidly. But on these instructive complications I must not enlarge more than to say that they could all be résuméd in the one word: Delay.

A mankind which has invented the proverb, 'Time is money,' will understand my vexation. The word 'Delay' entered the secret chamber of my brain, resounded there like a tolling bell which maddens the ear, affected all my senses, took on a black colouring, a bitter taste, a deadly meaning.

'I am really sorry to see you worried like this. Indeed, I am . . .'

It was the only humane speech I used to hear at that time. And it came from a doctor, appropriately enough.

A doctor is humane by definition. But that man was so in reality. His speech was not professional. I was not ill. But other people were and that was the reason of his visiting the ship.

He was the doctor of our Legation [15] and, of course, of the Consulate too. He looked after the ship's health, which generally was poor, and trembling, as it were, on the verge of a break-up. Yes. The men ailed. [16] And thus time was not only money, but life as well.

I have never seen such a steady ship's company. As the doctor remarked to me, 'You seem to have a most respectable lot of seamen.' Not only were they consistently sober, but they did not even want to go ashore. Care was taken to expose them as little as possible to the sun. They were employed on light work under the awnings. And the humane doctor commended me.

'Your arrangements appear to me to be very judicious, my dear Captain.'

It is difficult to express how much that pronouncement comforted me. The doctor's round full face framed in a light-coloured whisker was the perfection of a dignified amenity. He was the only human being in the world who seemed to take the slightest interest in me. He would generally sit in the cabin for half an hour or so at every visit.

I said to him one day:

'I suppose the only thing now is to take care of them as you are doing, till I can get the ship to sea?'

He inclined his head, shutting his eyes under the large spectacles, and murmured:

'The sea . . . undoubtedly.'

The first member of the crew fairly knocked over was the steward – the first man to whom I had spoken on board. He was taken ashore (with choleraic symptoms), and died there [17] at the end of a week. Then, while I was still under the startling impression of this first home-thrust of the climate, Mr Burns gave up and went to bed in a raging fever without saying a word to anybody.

I believe he had partly fretted himself into that illness; the climate did the rest with the swiftness of an invisible monster ambushed in the air, in the water, in the mud of the river-bank. Mr Burns was a predestined victim.

I discovered him lying on his back, glaring sullenly and radiating heat on one like a small furnace. He would hardly answer my questions, and only grumbled: Couldn't a man take an afternoon off duty with a bad headache – for once?

That evening, as I sat in the saloon after dinner, I could hear him muttering continuously in his room. Ransome, who was clearing the table, said to me:

'I am afraid, sir, I won't be able to give the mate all the attention he's likely to need. I will have to be forward in the galley a great part of my time.'

Ransome was the cook.[18] The mate had pointed him out to me the first day, standing on the deck, his arms crossed on his broad chest, gazing on the river.

Even at a distance his well-proportioned figure, something thoroughly sailor-like in his poise, made him noticeable. On nearer view the intelligent, quiet eyes, a well-bred face, the disciplined independence of his manner made up an attractive personality. When, in addition, Mr Burns told me that he was the best seaman in the ship, I expressed my surprise that in his earliest prime and of such appearance he should sign on as cook on board a ship.

'It's his heart,' Mr Burns had said. 'There's something wrong with it. He mustn't exert himself too much or he may drop dead suddenly.'

And he was the only one the climate had not touched – perhaps because, carrying a deadly enemy in his breast, he had schooled himself into a systematic control of feelings and movements. When one was in the secret this was apparent in his manner. After the poor steward died, and as he could not be replaced by a white man in this Oriental port, Ransome had volunteered to do the double work.

'I can do it all right, sir, as long as I go about it quietly,' he had assured me.

But obviously he couldn't be expected to take up sick-nursing in addition. Moreover, the doctor peremptorily ordered Mr Burns ashore.

With a seaman on each side holding him up under the arms, the mate went over the gangway more sullen than ever. We built him up with pillows in the gharry,[19] and he made an effort to say brokenly:

'Now – you've got – what you wanted – got me out of – the ship.'

'You were never more mistaken in your life, Mr Burns,' I said quietly, duly smiling at him; and the trap drove off to a sort of sanatorium, a pavilion of bricks which the doctor had in the grounds of his residence.

I visited Mr Burns regularly. After the first few days, when he didn't know anybody, he received me as if I had come either to gloat over a crushed enemy or else to curry favour with a deeply wronged person. It was either one or the other, just as it happened according to his fantastic sick-room moods. Whichever it was, he managed to convey it to me even during the period when he appeared almost too weak to talk. I treated him to my invariable kindliness.

Then one day, suddenly, a surge of downright panic burst through all this craziness.

If I left him behind in this deadly place he would die. He felt it, he was certain of it. But I wouldn't have the heart to leave him ashore. He had a wife and child in Sydney.

He produced his wasted forearms from under the sheet which covered him and clasped his fleshless claws. He would die! He would die here . . .

He absolutely managed to sit up, but only for a moment, and when he fell back I really thought that he would die there and then. I called to the Bengali dispenser, and hastened away from the room.

Next day he upset me thoroughly by renewing his entreaties. I returned an evasive answer, and left him the picture of ghastly despair. The day after I went in with reluctance, and he attacked me at once in a much stronger voice, and with an abundance of argument which was quite startling. He presented his case with a sort of crazy vigour, and asked me finally how would I like to have a man's death on my conscience? He wanted me to promise that I would not sail without him.

I said that I really must consult the doctor first. He cried out at that. The doctor! Never! That would be a death sentence.

The effort had exhausted him. He closed his eyes, but went on rambling in a low voice. I had hated him from the start. The late captain had hated him too. Had wished him dead. Had wished all hands dead . . .

'What do you want to stand in with that wicked corpse for, sir? He'll have you too,' he ended, blinking his glazed eyes vacantly.

'Mr Burns,' I cried, very much discomposed, 'what on earth are you talking about?'

He seemed to come to himself, though he was too weak to start. 'I don't know,' he said languidly. 'But don't ask that doctor, sir. You and I are sailors. Don't ask him, sir. Some day, perhaps, you will have a wife and child yourself.'

And again he pleaded for the promise that I would not leave him behind. I had the firmness of mind not to give it to him. Afterwards this sternness seemed criminal; for my mind was made up. That prostrated man, with hardly strength enough to breathe, and ravaged by a passion of fear, was irresistible. And, besides, he had happened to hit on the right words. He and I were sailors. That was a claim, for I had no other family. As to the wife-and-child (some day) argument, it had no force. It sounded merely bizarre.

I could imagine no claim that would be stronger and more absorbing than the claim of that ship, of these men snared in the river by silly commercial complications, as if in some poisonous trap.

However, I had nearly fought my way out. Out to sea. The sea – which was pure, safe, and friendly. Three days more.

That thought sustained and carried me on my way back to the ship. In the saloon the doctor's voice greeted me, and his large form followed his voice, issuing out of the starboard spare cabin [20] where the ship's medicine chest was kept securely lashed in the bed-place.

Finding that I was not on board he had gone in there, he said, to inspect the supply of drugs, bandages, and so on. Everything was completed and in order.

I thanked him; I had just been thinking of asking him to do that very thing, as in a couple of days, as he knew, we were going to sea, where all our troubles of every sort would be over at last.

He listened gravely and made no answer. But when I opened to him my mind as to Mr Burns, he sat down by my side, and, laying his hand on my knee amicably, begged me to think what it was I was exposing myself to.

The man was just strong enough to bear being moved, and no more. But he couldn't stand a return of the fever. I had before me a passage of sixty days, perhaps, beginning with intricate navigation and ending probably with a lot of bad weather. Could I run the risk of having to go through it single-handed, with no chief officer, and with a second quite a youth? . . .

He might have added that it was my first command, too. He did probably think of that fact, for he checked himself. It was very present to my mind.

He advised me earnestly to cable to Singapore for a chief officer, even if I had to delay my sailing for a week.

'Not a day,' I said. The very thought gave me the shivers. The hands seemed fairly fit, all of them, and this was the time to get them away. Once at sea I was not afraid of facing anything. The sea was now the only remedy for all my troubles.

The doctor's glasses were directed at me like two lamps searching the genuineness of my resolution. He opened his lips as if to argue further, but shut them again without saying anything. I had a vision of poor Burns so vivid in his exhaustion, helplessness, and anguish, that it moved me more than the reality I had come away from only an hour before. It was purged from the drawbacks of his personality, and I could not resist it.

'Look here,' I said, 'unless you tell me officially that the man must not be moved I'll make arrangements to have him brought on board tomorrow, and shall take the ship out of the river next morning, even if I have to anchor outside the bar for a couple of days to get her ready for sea.'

'Oh! I'll make all the arrangements myself,' said the doctor at once. 'I spoke as I did only as a friend – as a well-wisher, and that sort of thing.'

He rose in his dignified simplicity and gave me a warm hand-shake, rather solemnly, I thought. But he was as good as his word.

When Mr Burns appeared at the gangway, carried on a stretcher, the doctor himself walked by its side. The programme had been altered in so far that this transportation had been left to the last moment, on the very morning of our departure.

It was barely an hour after sunrise. The doctor waved his big arm to me from the shore and walked back at once to his trap, which had followed him empty to the riverside. Mr Burns, carried across the quarter-deck,[21] had the appearance of being absolutely lifeless. Ransome went down to settle him in his cabin. I had to remain on deck to look after the ship, for the tug had got hold of our tow-rope already.

The splash of our shore-fasts[22] falling in the water produced a complete change of feeling in me. It was like the imperfect relief of awakening from a nightmare. But when the ship's head swung down the river away from that town, Oriental and squalid, I missed the expected elation of that striven-for moment. What there was, undoubtedly, was a relaxation of tension which translated itself into a sense of weariness after an inglorious fight.

About midday we anchored a mile outside the bar. The afternoon was busy for all hands. Watching the work from the poop,[23] where I remained all the time, I detected in it some of the languor of the six weeks spent in the steaming heat of the river. The first breeze would blow that away. Now the calm was complete. I judged that the second officer[24] – a callow youth with an unpromising face – was not, to put it mildly, of that invaluable stuff from which a commander's right hand is made. But I was glad to catch along the main-deck a few smiles on those seamen's faces at which I had hardly had time to have a good look as yet. Having thrown off the mortal coil of shore affairs, I felt myself familiar with them, and yet a little strange, like a long-lost wanderer among his kin.

Ransome flitted continually to and fro between the galley and the cabin. It was a pleasure to look at him. The man positively had grace. He alone of all the crew had not had a day's illness in port. But with the knowledge of that uneasy heart within his breast I could detect the restraint he put on the natural sailor-like agility of his movements. It was as though he had something very fragile or very explosive to carry about his person, and was all the time aware of it.

I had occasion to address him once or twice. He answered me in his pleasant, quiet voice and with a faint, slightly wistful smile. Mr Burns appeared to be resting. He seemed fairly comfortable.

After sunset I came out on deck again to meet only a still void. The thin, featureless crust of the coast could not be distinguished. The darkness had risen around the ship like a mysterious emanation from the dumb and lonely waters. I leaned on the rail and turned my ear to the shadows of the night. Not a sound. My command might have been a planet flying vertiginously on its appointed path in a space of infinite silence. I clung to the rail as if my sense of balance were leaving me for good. How absurd. I hailed nervously.

'On deck there!'

The immediate answer, 'Yes, sir,' broke the spell. The anchor-watch man [25] ran up the poop ladder smartly. I told him to report at once the slightest sign of a breeze coming.

Going below I looked in on Mr Burns. In fact I could not avoid seeing him, for his door stood open. The man was so wasted that, in that white cabin, under a white sheet, with his diminished head sunk in the white pillow, his red moustaches captured one's eyes exclusively, like something artificial – a pair of moustaches from a shop exhibited there in the harsh light of the bulkhead-lamp [26] without a shade.

While I stared with a sort of wonder he asserted himself by opening his eyes and even moving them in my direction. A minute stir.

'Dead calm, Mr Burns,' I said resignedly.

In an unexpectedly distinct voice Mr Burns began a rambling speech. Its tone was very strange, not as if affected by his illness, but as if of a different nature. It sounded unearthly. As to the matter, I seemed to make out that it was the fault of the 'old man' – the late captain – ambushed down there under the sea with some evil intention. It was a weird story.

I listened to the end; then stepping into the cabin I laid my hand on the mate's forehead. It was cool. He was light-headed only from extreme weakness. Suddenly he seemed to become aware of me, and in his own voice – of course, very feeble – he asked regretfully:

'Is there no chance at all to get under way, sir?'

'What's the good of letting go our hold of the ground only to drift, Mr Burns?' I answered.

He sighed, and I left him to his immobility. His hold on life was as slender as his hold on sanity. I was oppressed by my lonely responsibilities. I went into my cabin to seek relief in a few hours' sleep, but almost before I closed my eyes the man on deck came down reporting a light breeze. Enough to get under way with, he said.

And it was not more than just enough. I ordered the windlass[27] manned, the sails loosed, and the topsails set. But by the time I had cast the ship I could hardly feel any breath of wind. Nevertheless, I trimmed the yards[28] and put everything on her. I was not going to give up the attempt.

CHAPTER FOUR

With her anchor at the bow, and clothed in canvas to her very trucks, my command seemed to stand as motionless as a model ship set on the gleams and shadows of polished marble. It was impossible to distinguish land from water in the enigmatical tranquillity of the immense forces of the world. A sudden impatience possessed me.

'Won't she answer the helm at all?' I said irritably to the man whose strong brown hands grasping the spokes of the wheel stood out lighted on the darkness – like a symbol of mankind's claim to the direction of its own fate.

He answered me:

'Yes, sir. She's coming-to slowly.'

'Let her head come up to south.'

'Aye, aye, sir.'

I paced the poop. There was not a sound but that of my footsteps, till the man spoke again:

'She is at south now, sir.'

I felt a slight tightness of the chest before I gave out the first course of my first command to the silent night, heavy with dew and sparkling with stars. There was a finality in the act committing me to the endless vigilance of my lonely task.

'Steady her head at that,' I said at last. 'The course is south.'

'South, sir,' echoed the man.

I sent below the second mate and his watch and remained in charge, walking the deck through the chill, somnolent hours that precede the dawn.

Slight puffs came and went, and whenever they were strong enough to wake up the black water the murmur alongside ran through my very heart in a delicate crescendo of delight, and died away swiftly. I was bitterly tired. The very stars seemed weary of waiting for daybreak. It came at last with a mother-of-pearl sheen at the zenith, such as I had never seen before in the tropics, unglowing, almost grey, with a strange reminder of high latitudes.

The voice of the look-out man hailed from forward:

'Land on the port bow,[1] sir.'

'All right.'

Leaning on the rail I never even raised my eyes. The motion of the ship was imperceptible. Presently Ransome brought me the cup of morning coffee. After I had drunk it I looked ahead, and in the still streak of very bright pale orange light I saw the land profiled flatly, as if cut out of black paper, and seeming to float on the water as light as cork. But the rising sun turned it into mere dark vapour, a doubtful, massive shadow trembling in the hot glare.

The watch finished washing decks. I went below, and stopped at Mr Burns's door (he could not bear to have it shut), but hesitated to speak to him till he moved his eyes. I gave him the news.

'Sighted Cape Liant[2] at daylight. About fifteen miles.'

He moved his lips then, but I heard no sound till I put my ear down, and caught the peevish comment, 'This is crawling ... No luck.'

'Better luck than standing still, anyhow,' I pointed out resignedly, and left him to whatever thoughts or fancies haunted his hopeless prostration.

Later that morning, when relieved by my second officer, I threw myself on my couch, and for some three hours or so I really found oblivion. It was so perfect that on waking up I wondered where I was. Then came the immense relief of the thought: on board my ship! At sea! At sea!

Through the port-holes I beheld an unruffled, sun-smitten horizon: the horizon of a windless day. But its spaciousness alone was enough to give me a sense of a fortunate escape, a momentary exultation of freedom.

I stepped out into the saloon with my heart lighter than it had been for days. Ransome was at the sideboard preparing to lay the table for the first sea dinner of the passage. He turned his head, and something in his eyes checked my modest elation.

Instinctively I asked, 'What is it now?' not expecting in the least the answer I got. It was given with that sort of contained serenity which was characteristic of the man.

'I am afraid we haven't left all sickness behind us, sir.'

'We haven't? What's the matter?'

He told me then that two of our men had been taken bad with fever in the night. One of them was burning and the other was shivering, but he thought that it was pretty much the same thing. I thought so too. I felt shocked by the news. 'One burning, the other shivering, you say? No. We haven't left the sickness behind. Do they look very ill?'

'Middling bad, sir.' Ransome's eyes gazed steadily into mine. We exchanged smiles. Ransome's a little wistful, as usual, mine no doubt grim enough, to correspond with my secret exasperation.

I asked:

'Was there any wind at all this morning?'

'Can hardly say that, sir. We've moved all the time, though. The land ahead seems a little nearer.'

That was it. A little nearer. Whereas if we had only had a little more wind, only a very little more, we might, we should, have been abreast of Liant by this time, and increasing our distance from that contaminated shore. And it was not only the distance. It seemed to me that a stronger breeze would have blown away the infection which clung to the ship. It obviously did cling to the ship. Two men. One burning, one shivering. I felt a distinct reluctance to go and look at them. What was the good? Poison is poison. Tropical fever is tropical fever. But that it should have stretched its claw after us over the sea seemed to me an extraordinary and unfair licence. I could hardly believe that it could be anything worse than the last desperate pluck of the evil from which we were escaping into the clean breath of the sea. If only that breath had been a little stronger. However, there was the quinine against the fever. I went into the spare cabin, where the medicine chest was kept, to prepare two doses. I opened it full of faith as a man opens a miraculous shrine. The upper part was inhabited by a collection of bottles, all square-shouldered, and as like each other as peas. Under that orderly array there were two drawers, stuffed as full of things as one could imagine – paper packages, bandages, cardboard boxes officially labelled. The lower of the two, in one of its compartments, contained our provision of quinine.

There were five bottles, all round and all of a size. One was about a third full. The other four remained still wrapped up in paper and sealed. But I did not expect to see an envelope lying on top of them – a square envelope belonging, in fact, to the ship's stationery.

It lay so that I could see it was not closed down, and on picking it up and turning it over I perceived that it was addressed to myself. It contained a half-sheet of notepaper, which I unfolded with a queer sense of dealing with the uncanny, but without any excitement as people meet and do extraordinary things in a dream.

'My dear captain,' it began, but I ran to the signature. The writer was the doctor. The date was that of the day on which, returning from my visit to Mr Burns in the hospital, I had found the excellent doctor waiting for me in the cabin; and when he told me that he had been putting in time inspecting the medicine chest for me. How bizarre! While expecting me to come in at any moment he had been amusing himself by writing me a letter, and then as I came in had hastened to stuff it into the medicine-chest drawer. A rather incredible proceeding. I turned to the text in wonder.

In a large, hurried, but legible hand the good, sympathetic man for some reason, either of kindness or more likely impelled by the irresistible desire to express his opinion, with which he didn't want to damp my hopes before, was warning me not to put my trust in the beneficial effects of a change from land to sea. 'I didn't want to add to your worries by discouraging your hopes,' he wrote. 'I am afraid that, medically speaking, the end of your troubles is not yet.' In short, he expected me to have to fight a probable return of tropical illness. Fortunately I had a good provision of quinine. I should put my trust in that, and administer it steadily, when the ship's health would certainly improve.

I crumpled up the letter and rammed it into my pocket. Ransome carried off two big doses to the men forward. As to myself, I did not go on deck as yet. I went instead to the door of Mr Burns's room, and gave him that news, too.

It was impossible to say the effect it had on him. At first I thought that he was speechless. His head lay sunk in the pillow. He moved his lips enough, however, to assure me that he was getting much stronger; a statement shockingly untrue on the face of it.

That afternoon I took my watch as a matter of course. A great overheated stillness enveloped the ship, and seemed to hold her motionless in a flaming ambience composed in two shades of blue. Faint, hot puffs eddied nervelessly from her sails. And yet she moved. She must have. For, as the sun was setting, we had drawn abreast of Cape Liant and dropped it behind us: an ominous retreating shadow in the last gleams of twilight.

In the evening, under the crude glare of his lamp, Mr Burns seemed to have come more to the surface of his bedding. It was as if a depressing hand had been lifted off him. He answered my few words by a comparatively long, connected speech. He asserted himself strongly. If he escaped being smothered by this stagnant heat, he said, he was confident that in a very few days he would be able to come up on deck and help me.

While he was speaking I trembled lest this effort of energy should leave him lifeless before my eyes. But I cannot deny that there was something comforting in his willingness. I made a suitable reply, but pointed out to him that the only thing that could really help us was wind – a fair wind.

He rolled his head impatiently on the pillow. And it was not comforting in the least to hear him begin to mutter crazily about the late captain, that old man buried in latitude 8° 20′, right in our way – ambushed at the entrance of the Gulf.

'Are you still thinking of your late captain, Mr Burns?' I said. 'I imagine the dead feel no animosity against the living. They care nothing for them.'

'You don't know that one,' he breathed out feebly.

'No. I didn't know him, and he didn't know me. And so he can't have any grievance against me, anyway.'

'Yes. But there's all the rest of us on board,' he insisted.

I felt the inexpugnable strength of common sense being insidiously menaced by this gruesome, by this insane, delusion. And I said:

'You mustn't talk so much. You will tire yourself.'

'And there is the ship herself,' he persisted in a whisper.

'Now, not a word more,' I said, stepping in and laying my hand on his cool forehead. It proved to me that this atrocious absurdity was rooted in the man himself and not in the disease, which, apparently, had emptied him of every power, mental and physical, except that one fixed idea.

I avoided giving Mr Burns any opening for conversation for the next few days. I merely used to throw him a hasty, cheery word when passing his door. I believe that if he had had the strength he would have called out after me more than once. But he hadn't the strength. Ransome, however, observed to me one afternoon that the mate 'seemed to be picking up wonderfully.'

'Did he talk any nonsense to you of late?' I asked casually.

'No, sir.' Ransome was startled by the direct question; but, after a pause, he added equably, 'He told me this morning, sir, that he was sorry he had to bury our late captain right in the ship's way, as one may say, out of the Gulf.'

'Isn't this nonsense enough for you?' I asked, looking confidently at the intelligent, quiet face on which the secret uneasiness in the man's breast had thrown a transparent veil of care.

Ransome didn't know. He had not given a thought to the matter. And with a faint smile he flitted away from me on his never-ending duties, with his usual guarded activity.

Two more days passed. We had advanced a little way – a very little way – into the larger space of the Gulf of Siam. Seizing eagerly upon the elation of the first command thrown into my lap, by the agency of Captain Giles, I had yet an uneasy feeling that such luck as this has got, perhaps, to be paid for in some way. I had held, professionally, a review of my chances. I was competent enough for that. At least I thought so. I had a general sense of my preparedness which only a man pursuing a calling he loves can know. That feeling seemed to me the most natural thing in the world. As natural as breathing. I imagined I could not have lived without it.

I don't know what I expected. Perhaps nothing else than that special intensity of existence which is the quintessence of youthful aspirations. Whatever I expected I did not expect to be beset by hurricanes. I knew better than that. In the Gulf of Siam there are no hurricanes. But neither did I expect to find myself bound hand and foot to the hopeless extent which was revealed to me as the days went on.

Not that the evil spell held us always motionless. Mysterious currents drifted us here and there, with a stealthy power made manifest by the changing vistas of the islands fringing the east shore of the Gulf. And there were winds, too, fitful and deceitful. They raised hopes only to dash them into the bitterest disappointment, promises of advance ending in lost ground, expiring in sighs, dying into dumb stillness in which the currents had it all their own way – their own inimical way.

The Island of Koh-ring,[3] a great, black, upheaved ridge amongst a lot of tiny islets, lying upon the glassy water like a triton amongst minnows, seemed to be the centre of the fatal circle. It seemed impossible to get away from it. Day after day it remained in sight. More than once, in a favourable breeze, I would take its bearing in the fast-ebbing twilight, thinking that it was for the last time. Vain hope. A night of fitful airs would undo the gains of temporary favour, and the rising sun would throw out the black relief of Koh-ring, looking more barren, inhospitable, and grim than ever.

'It's like being bewitched, upon my word.' I said once to Mr Burns, from my usual position in the doorway.

He was sitting up in his bed-place. He was progressing towards the world of living men – if he could hardly have been said to have rejoined it yet. He nodded to me his frail and bony head in a wisely mysterious assent.

'Oh yes, I know what you mean,' I said. 'But you cannot expect me to believe that a dead man has the power to put out of joint the meteorology of this part of the world. Though, indeed, it seems to have gone utterly wrong. The land and sea breezes have got broken up into small pieces. We cannot depend upon them for five minutes together.'

'It won't be very long now before I can come up on deck,' muttered Mr Burns; 'and then we shall see.'

Whether he meant this for a promise to grapple with supernatural evil I couldn't tell. At any rate, it wasn't the kind of assistance I needed. On the other hand, I had been living on deck practically night and day so as to take advantage of every chance to get my ship a little more to the southward. The mate, I could see, was extremely weak yet, and not quite rid of his delusion, which to me appeared but a symptom of his disease. At all events, the hopefulness of an invalid was not to be discouraged. I said:

'You will be most welcome there, I am sure, Mr Burns. If you go on improving at this rate you'll be presently one of the healthiest men in the ship.'

This pleased him, but his extreme emaciation converted his self-satisfied smile into a ghastly exhibition of long teeth under the red moustache.

'Aren't the fellows improving, sir?' he asked soberly, with an extremely sensible expression of anxiety on his face.

I answered him only with a vague gesture, and went away from the door. The fact was that disease played with us capriciously very much as the winds did. It would go from one man to another with a lighter or heavier touch, which always left its mark behind, staggering some, knocking others over for a time, leaving this one, returning to another, so that all of them had now an invalidish aspect and a hunted, apprehensive look in their eyes; while Ransome and I, the only two completely untouched, went amongst them assiduously distributing quinine. It was a double fight. The adverse weather held us in front, and the disease pressed on our rear. I must say that the men were very good. The constant toil of trimming the yards they faced willingly. But all spring was out of their limbs, and as I looked at them from the poop I could not keep from my mind the dreadful impression that they were moving in poisoned air.

Down below, in his cabin, Mr Burns had advanced so far as not only to be able to sit up, but even to draw up his legs. Clasping them with bony arms, like an animated skeleton, he emitted deep, impatient sighs.

'The great thing to do, sir,' he would tell me on every occasion, when I gave him the chance, 'the great thing is to get the ship past 8° 20′ of latitude. Once she's past that we're all right.'

At first I used only to smile at him, though, God knows, I had not much heart left for smiles. But at last I lost my patience.

'Oh yes. The latitude 8° 20′. That's where you buried your late captain, isn't it?' Then with severity, 'Don't you think, Mr Burns, it's about time you dropped all that nonsense?'

He rolled at me his deep-sunken eyes in a glance of invincible obstinacy. But for the rest, he only muttered, just loud enough for me to hear, something about 'Not surprised ... find ... play us some beastly trick yet ...'

Such passages as this were not exactly wholesome for my resolution. The stress of adversity was beginning to tell on me. At the same time I felt a contempt for that obscure weakness of my soul. I said to myself disdainfully that it should take much more than that to affect in the smallest degree my fortitude.

I didn't know then how soon and from what unexpected direction it would be attacked.

It was the very next day. The sun had risen clear of the southern shoulder of Koh-ring, which still hung, like an evil attendant, on our port quarter. It was intensely hateful to my sight. During the night we had been heading all round the compass, trimming the yards again and again, to what I fear must have been for the most part imaginary puffs of air. Then just about sunrise we got for an hour an inexplicable, steady breeze, right in our teeth. There was no sense in it. It fitted neither with the season of the year, nor with the secular experience of seamen as recorded in books, nor with the aspect of the sky. Only purposeful malevolence could account for it. It sent us travelling at a great pace away from our proper course; and if we had been out on pleasure sailing bent it would have been a delightful breeze, with the awakened sparkle of the sea, with the sense of motion and a feeling of unwonted freshness. Then all at once, as if disdaining to carry farther the sorry jest, it dropped and died out completely in less than five minutes. The ship's head swung where it listed; the stilled sea took on the polish of a steel plate in the calm.

I went below, not because I meant to take some rest, but simply because I couldn't bear to look at it just then. The indefatigable Ransome was busy in the saloon. It had become a regular practice with him to give me an informal health report in the morning. He turned away from the sideboard with his usual pleasant, quiet gaze. No shadow rested on his intelligent forehead.

'There are a good many of them middling bad this morning, sir,' he said in a calm tone.

'What? All knocked out?'

'Only two actually in their bunks, sir, but . . .'

'It's the last night that has done for them. We have had to pull and haul all the blessed time.'

'I heard, sir. I had a mind to come out and help, only, you know ...'

'Certainly not. You mustn't ... The fellows lie at night about the decks, too. It isn't good for them.'

Ransome assented. But men couldn't be looked after like children. Moreover, one could hardly blame them for trying for such coolness and such air as there were to be found on deck. He himself, of course, knew better.

He was, indeed, a reasonable man. Yet it would have been hard to say that the others were not. The last few days had been for us like the ordeal of the fiery furnace. One really couldn't quarrel with their common, imprudent humanity making the best of the moments of relief, when the night brought in the illusion of coolness and the starlight twinkled through the heavy, dew-laden air. Moreover, most of them were so weakened that hardly anything could be done without everybody that could totter mustering on the braces.[4] No, it was no use remonstrating with them. But I fully believed that quinine was of very great use indeed.

I believed in it. I pinned my faith to it. It would save the men, the ship, break the spell by its medicinal virtue, make time of no account, the weather but a passing worry, and, like a magic powder working against mysterious malefices, secure the first passage of my first command against the evil powers of calm and pestilence. I looked upon it as more precious than gold, and unlike gold, of which there hardly ever seems to be enough anywhere, the ship had a sufficient store of it. I went in to get it with the purpose of weighing out doses. I stretched my hand with the feeling of a man reaching for an unfailing panacea, took up a fresh bottle and unrolled the wrapper, noticing as I did so that the ends, both top and bottom, had come unsealed ...

But why record all the swift steps of the appalling discovery? You have guessed the truth already. There was the wrapper, the bottle, and the white powder inside, some sort of powder! But it wasn't quinine. One look at it was quite enough. I remember that at the very moment of picking up the bottle, before I even dealt with the wrapper, the weight of the object I had in my hand gave me an instant of premonition. Quinine is as light as feathers; and my nerves must have been exasperated into an extraordinary sensibility. I let the bottle smash itself on the floor. The stuff, whatever it was, felt gritty under the sole of my shoe. I snatched up the next bottle and then the next. The weight alone told the tale. One after another they fell, breaking at my feet, not because I threw them down in dismay, but slipping through my fingers as if this disclosure was too much for my strength.

It is a fact that the very greatness of a mental shock helps one to bear up against it, by producing a sort of temporary insensibility. I came out of the state-room stunned, as if something heavy had dropped on my head. From the other side of the saloon, across the table, Ransome, with a duster in his hand, stared open-mouthed. I don't think that I looked wild. It is quite possible that I appeared to be in a hurry, because I was instinctively hastening up on deck. An example this of training become instinct. The difficulties, the dangers, the problems of a ship at sea must be met on deck.

To this fact, as it were of nature, I responded instinctively; which may be taken as a proof that for a moment I must have been robbed of my reason.

I was certainly off my balance, a prey to impulse, for at the bottom of the stairs I turned and flung myself at the doorway of Mr Burns's cabin. The wildness of his aspect checked my mental disorder. He was sitting up in his bunk, his body looking immensely long, his head drooping a little sideways, with affected complacency. He flourished, in his trembling hand, on the end of a forearm no thicker than a stout walking-stick, a shining pair of scissors which he tried before my very eyes to jab at his throat.

I was to a certain extent horrified; but it was rather a secondary sort of effect, not really strong enough to make me yell at him in some such manner as, 'Stop!' ... 'Heavens!' ... 'What are you doing?'

In reality he was simply overtaxing his returning strength in a shaky attempt to clip off the thick growth of his red beard. A large towel was spread over his lap, and a shower of stiff hairs, like bits of copper wire, was descending on it at every snip of the scissors.

He turned to me his face grotesque beyond the fantasies of mad dreams, one cheek all bushy as if with a swollen flame, the other denuded and sunken, with the untouched long moustache on that side asserting itself, lonely and fierce. And while he stared thunderstruck, with the gaping scissors on his fingers, I shouted my discovery at him fiendishly, in six words, without comment.

CHAPTER FIVE

I heard the clatter of the scissors escaping from his hand, noted the perilous heave of his whole person over the edge of the bunk after them, and then, returning to my first purpose, pursued my course on to the deck. The sparkle of the sea filled my eyes. It was gorgeous and barren, monotonous and without hope under the empty curve of the sky. The sails hung motionless and slack, the very folds of their sagging surfaces moved no more than carved granite. The impetuosity of my advent made the man at the helm start slightly. A block aloft squeaked incomprehensibly, for what on earth could have made it do so? It was a whistling note like a bird's. For a long, long time I faced an empty world, steeped in an infinity of silence, through which the sunshine poured and flowed for some mysterious purpose. Then I heard Ransome's voice at my elbow.

'I have put Mr Burns back to bed, sir.'

'You have?'

'Well, sir, he got out all of a sudden, but when he let go of the edge of his bunk he fell down. He isn't light-headed, though. it seems to me.'

'No,' I said dully, without looking at Ransome. He waited for a moment, then, cautiously as if not to give offence: 'I don't think we need lose much of that stuff, sir,' he said. 'I can sweep it up. every bit of it almost, and then we could sift the glass out. I will go about it at once. It will not make the breakfast late, not ten minutes.'

'Oh yes,' I said bitterly. 'Let the breakfast wait, sweep up every bit of it, and then throw the damned lot overboard!'

The profound silence returned, and when I looked over my shoulder Ransome – the intelligent, serene Ransome – had vanished from my side. The intense loneliness of the sea acted like poison on my brain. When I turned my eyes to the ship, I had a morbid vision of her as a floating grave. Who hasn't heard of ships found drifting, haphazard, with their crews all dead? [1] I looked at the seaman at the helm, I had an impulse to speak to him, and, indeed, his face took on an expectant cast as if he had guessed my intention. But in the end I went below, thinking I would be alone with the greatness of my trouble for a little while. But through his open door Mr Burns saw me come down, and addressed me grumpily, 'Well, sir?'

I went in. 'It isn't well at all,' I said.

Mr Burns, re-established in his bed-place, was concealing his hirsute cheek in the palm of his hand.

'That confounded fellow has taken away the scissors from me,' were the next words he said.

The tension I was suffering from was so great that it was perhaps just as well that Mr Burns had started on this grievance. He seemed very sore about it, and grumbled, 'Does he think I am mad, or what?'

'I don't think so, Mr Burns,' I said. I looked upon him at that moment as a model of self-possession. I even conceived on that account a sort of admiration for that man, who had (apart from the intense materiality of what was left of his beard) come as near to being a disembodied spirit as any man can do, and live. I noticed the preternatural sharpness of the ridge of his nose, the deep cavities of his temples, and I envied him. He was so reduced that he would probably die very soon. Enviable man! So near extinction – while I had to bear within me a tumult of suffering vitality, doubt, confusion, self-reproach, and an indefinite reluctance to meet the horrid logic of the situation. I could not help muttering, 'I feel as if I were going mad myself.'

Mr Burns glared spectrally, but otherwise wonderfully composed.

'I always thought he would play us some deadly trick,' he said, with a peculiar emphasis on the *he*.

It gave me a mental shock, but I had neither the mind, nor the heart, nor the spirit to argue with him. My form of sickness was indifference – the creeping paralysis of a hopeless outlook. So I only gazed at him. Mr Burns broke into further speech:

'Eh? What? No! You won't believe it? Well, how do you account for this? How do you think it could have happened?'

'Happened?' I repeated dully. 'Why, yes, how in the name of the infernal powers did this thing happen?'

Indeed, on thinking it out, it seemed incomprehensible that it should just be like this: the bottles emptied, refilled, rewrapped, and replaced. A sort of plot, a sinister attempt to deceive, a thing resembling sly vengeance – but for what? – or else a fiendish joke. But Mr Burns was in possession of a theory. It was simple, and he uttered it solemnly in a hollow voice.

'I suppose they have given him about fifteen pounds in Haiphong for that little lot.'

'Mr Burns!' I cried.

He nodded grotesquely over his raised legs, like two broomsticks in the pyjamas, with enormous bare feet at the end.

'Why not? The stuff is pretty expensive in this part of the world, and they were very short of it in Tongkin.[2] And what did he care? You have not known him. I have, and I have defied him. He feared neither God, nor devil, nor man, nor wind, nor sea, nor his own conscience. And I believe he hated everybody and everything. But I think he was afraid to die. I believe I am the only man who ever stood up to him. I faced him in that cabin where you live now, when he was sick, and I cowed him then. He thought I was going to twist his neck for him. If he had had his way we would have been beating up against the North-East monsoon, as long as he lived and afterwards too, for ages and ages. Acting the Flying Dutchman in the China Sea! Ha, ha!'

'But why should he replace the bottles like this? . . .' I began.

'Why shouldn't he? Why should he want to throw the bottles away? They fit the drawer. They belong to the medicine chest.'

'And they were wrapped up,' I cried.

'Well, the wrappers were there. Did it from habit, I suppose, and as to refilling, there is always a lot of stuff they send in paper parcels that burst after a time. And then, who can tell? I suppose you didn't taste it, sir? But, of course, you are sure . . .'

'No,' I said. 'I didn't taste it. It is all overboard now.'

Behind me, a soft, cultivated voice said, 'I have tasted it. It seemed a mixture of all sorts, sweetish, saltish, very horrible.'

Ransome, stepping out of the pantry, had been listening for some time, as it was very excusable in him to do.

'A dirty trick,' said Mr Burns. 'I always said he would.'

The magnitude of my indignation was unbounded. And the

kind, sympathetic doctor, too. The only sympathetic man I ever knew . . . instead of writing that warning letter, the very refinement of sympathy, why didn't the man make a proper inspection? But, as a matter of fact, it was hardly fair to blame the doctor. The fittings were in order, and the medicine chest is an officially arranged affair. There was nothing really to arouse the slightest suspicion. The person I could never forgive was myself. Nothing should ever be taken for granted. The seed of everlasting remorse was sown in my breast.

'I feel it's all my fault,' I exclaimed, 'mine, and nobody else's. That's how I feel. I shall never forgive myself.'

'That's very foolish, sir,' said Mr Burns fiercely.

And after this effort he fell back exhausted on his bed. He closed his eyes, he panted; this affair, this abominable surprise had shaken him up, too. As I turned away I perceived Ransome looking at me blankly. He appreciated what it meant, but he managed to produce his pleasant, wistful smile. Then he stepped back into his pantry, and I rushed up on deck again to see whether there was any wind, any breath under the sky, any stir of the air, any sign of hope. The deadly stillness met me again. Nothing was changed, except that there was a different man at the wheel. He looked ill. His whole figure drooped, and he seemed rather to cling to the spokes than hold them with a controlling grip. I said to him:

'You are not fit to be here.'

'I can manage, sir,' he said feebly.

As a matter of fact, there was nothing for him to do. The ship had no steerage way. She lay with her head to the westward, the everlasting Koh-ring visible over the stern, with a few small islets, black spots in the great blaze, swimming before my troubled eyes. And but for those bits of land there was no speck on the sky, no speck on the water, no shape of vapour, no wisp of smoke, no sail, no boat, no stir of humanity, no sign of life, nothing!

The first question was, what to do? What could one do? The first thing to do obviously was to tell the men. I did it that very day. I wasn't going to let the knowledge simply get about. I would face them. They were assembled on the quarter-deck for the purpose. Just before I stepped out to speak to them I discovered that life could hold terrible moments. No confessed criminal had ever been so oppressed by his sense of guilt. This is why, perhaps, my face was set hard and my voice curt and unemotional while I made my declaration that I could do nothing more for the sick, in the way of drugs. As to such care as could be given them they knew they had had it.

I would have held them justified in tearing me limb from limb. The silence which followed upon my words was almost harder to bear than the angriest uproar. I was crushed by the infinite depths of its reproach. But, as a matter of fact, I was mistaken. In a voice which I had great difficulty in keeping firm, I went on: 'I suppose, men, you have understood what I said, and you know what it means?'

A voice or two were heard: 'Yes, sir . . . We understand.'

They had kept silent simply because they thought that they were not called upon to say anything; and when I told them that I intended to run into Singapore, and that the best chance for the ship and the men was in the efforts all of us, sick and well, must make to get her along out of this, I received the encouragement of a low, assenting murmur and of a louder voice exclaiming, 'Surely there is a way out of this blamed hole.'

Here is an extract from the notes I wrote at the time.

'We have lost Koh-ring at last. For many days now I don't think I have been two hours below altogether. I remain on deck, of course, night and day, and the nights and the days wheel over us in succession, whether long or short, who can say? All sense of time is lost in the monotony of expectation, of hope, and of desire – which is only one: Get the ship to the southward! Get the ship to the southward! The effect is curiously mechanical; the sun climbs and descends, the night swings over our heads as if somebody below the horizon were turning a crank. It is the pettiest, the most aimless! . . . and all through that miserable performance I go on, tramping, tramping the deck. How many miles have I walked on the poop of that ship! A stubborn pilgrimage of sheer restlessness, diversified by short excursions below to look upon Mr Burns. I don't know whether it is an illusion, but he seems to become more substantial from day to day. He doesn't say much, for, indeed, the situation doesn't lend itself to idle remarks. I notice this even with the men as I watch them moving or sitting about the decks. They don't talk to each other. It strikes me that if there exist an invisible ear catching the whispers of the earth, it will find this ship the most silent spot on it . . .

'No, Mr Burns has not much to say to me. He sits in his bunk with his beard gone, his moustaches flaming, and with an air of silent determination on his chalky physiognomy. Ransome tells me he devours all the food that is given him to the last scrap, but that, apparently, he sleeps very little. Even at night, when I go below to fill my pipe, I notice that, though dozing flat on his back, he still looks very determined. From the side glance he gives me when awake it seems as though he were annoyed at being inter-rupted in some arduous mental operation; and as I emerge on deck the ordered arrangement of the stars meets my eyes, unclouded, infinitely wearisome. There they are: stars, sun, sea, light, dark-ness, space, great waters; the formidable Work of the Seven Days, into which mankind seems to have blundered unbidden. Or else decoyed. Even as I have been decoyed into this awful, this death-haunted command . . .'

The only spot of light in the ship at night was that of the com-pass-lamps, lighting up the faces of the succeeding helmsmen; for the rest we were lost in the darkness, I walking the poop and the men lying about the decks. They were all so reduced by sickness that no watches could be kept. Those who were able to walk remained all the time on duty, lying about in the shadows of the main-deck, till my voice raised for an order would bring them to their enfeebled feet, a tottering little group, moving patiently about the ship, with hardly a murmur, a whisper amongst them all. And every time I had to raise my voice it was with a pang of remorse and pity.

Then about four o'clock in the morning a light would gleam forward in the galley. The unfailing Ransome with the uneasy heart, immune, serene, and active, was getting ready the early coffee for the men. Presently he would bring me a cup up on the poop, and it was then that I allowed myself to drop into my deck-chair for a couple of hours of real sleep. No doubt I must have been snatching short dozes when leaning against the rail for a moment in sheer exhaustion; but, honestly, I was not aware of them, except in the painful form of convulsive starts that seemed to come on me even while I walked. From about five, however, until after seven I would sleep openly under the fading stars.

I would say to the helmsman, 'Call me at need,' and drop into that chair and close my eyes, feeling that there was no more sleep for me on earth. And then I would know nothing till, some time between seven and eight, I would feel a touch on my shoulder and look up at Ransome's face, with its faint, wistful smile and friendly grey eyes, as though he were tenderly amused at my slumbers. Occasionally the second mate would come up and relieve me at early coffee-time. But it didn't really matter. Generally it was a dead calm, or else faint airs so changing and fugitive that it really wasn't worth while to touch a brace for them. If the air steadied at all the seaman at the helm could be trusted for a warning shout: 'Ship's all aback,³ sir!' which like a trumpet-call would make me spring a foot above the deck. Those were the words which it seemed to me would have made me spring up from eternal sleep. But this was not often. I have never met since such breathless sunrises. And if the second mate happened to be there (he had generally one day in three free of fever) I would find him sitting on the skylight half-senseless, as it were, and with an idiotic gaze fastened on some object near by – a rope, a cleat, a belaying pin, a ring-bolt.⁴

That young man was rather troublesome. He remained cubbish in his sufferings. He seemed to have become completely imbecile; and when the return of fever drove him to his cabin below, the next thing would be that we would miss him from there. The first time it happened Ransome and I were very much alarmed. We started a quiet search, and ultimately Ransome discovered him curled up in the sail-locker, which opened into the lobby by a sliding door. When remonstrated with he muttered sulkily, 'It's cool in there.' That wasn't true. It was only dark there.

The fundamental defects of his face were not improved by its uniform livid hue. It was not so with many of the men. The wastage of ill-health seemed to idealise the general character of the features, bringing out the unsuspected nobility of some, the strength of others and in one case revealing an essentially comic aspect. He was a short, gingery, active man with a nose and chin of the Punch type, and whom his shipmates called 'Frenchy,'[5] I don't know why. He may have been a Frenchman, but I have never heard him utter a single word in French.

To see him coming aft to the wheel comforted one. The blue dungaree trousers turned up the calf, one leg a little higher than the other, the clean check shirt, the white canvas cap, evidently made by himself, made up a whole of peculiar smartness, and the persistent jauntiness of his gait, even, poor fellow, when he couldn't help tottering, told of his invincible spirit. There was also a man called Gambril.[6] He was the only grizzled person in the ship. His face was of an austere type. But if I remember all their faces, wasting tragically before my eyes, most of their names have vanished from my memory.

The words that passed between us were few and puerile in regard to the situation. I had to force myself to look them in the face. I expected to meet reproachful glances. There were none. The expression of suffering in their eyes was indeed hard enough to bear. But that they couldn't help. For the rest, I ask myself whether it was the temper of their souls or the sympathy of their imagination that made them so wonderful, so worthy of my undying regard.

For myself, neither my soul was highly tempered, nor my imagination properly under control. There were moments when I felt, not only that I would go mad, but that I had gone mad already; so that I dared not open my lips for fear of betraying myself by some insane shriek. Luckily I had only orders to give, and an order has a steadying influence upon him who has to give it. Moreover, the seaman, the officer of the watch, in me was sufficiently sane. I was like a mad carpenter making a box. Were he ever so convinced that he was King of Jerusalem, the box he would make would be a sane box. What I feared was a shrill note escaping me involuntarily, and upsetting my balance. Luckily, again, there was no necessity to raise one's voice. The brooding stillness of the world seemed sensitive to the slightest sound like a whispering gallery. The conversational tone would almost carry a word from one end of the ship to the other. The terrible thing was that the only voice that I ever heard was my own. At night especially it reverberated very lonely amongst the planes of the unstirring sails.

Mr Burns, still keeping to his bed with that air of secret determination, was moved to grumble at many things. Our interviews were short five-minute affairs, but fairly frequent. I was everlastingly diving down below to get a light, though I did not consume much tobacco at that time. The pipe was always going out; for in truth my mind was not composed enough to enable me to get a decent smoke. Likewise, for most of the time during the twenty-four hours I could have struck matches on deck and held them aloft till the flame burnt my fingers. But I always used to run below. It was a change. It was the only break in the incessant strain; and, of course, Mr Burns through the open door could see me come in and go out every time.

With his knees gathered up under his chin, and staring with his greenish eyes over them, he was a weird figure, and with my knowledge of the crazy notion in his head, not a very attractive one for me. Still, I had to speak to him now and then, and one day he complained that the ship was very silent. For hours and hours, he said, he was lying there, not hearing a sound, till he did not know what to do with himself.

'When Ransome happens to be forward in his galley everything's so still that one might think everybody in the ship was dead,' he grumbled. 'The only voice I do hear sometimes is yours, sir, and that isn't enough to cheer me up. What's the matter with the men? Isn't there one left that can sing out at the ropes?'

'Not one, Mr Burns,' I said. 'There is no breath to spare on board this ship for that. Are you aware that there are times when I can't muster more than three hands to do anything?'

He asked swiftly but fearfully:

'Nobody dead yet, sir?'

'No.'

'It wouldn't do,' Mr Burns declared forcibly. 'Mustn't let him. If he gets hold of one he will get them all.'

I cried out angrily at this. I believe I even swore at the disturbing effect of these words. They attacked all the self-possession that was left to me. In my endless vigil in the face of the enemy I had been haunted by gruesome images enough. I had had visions of a ship drifting in calms and swinging in light airs, with all her crew dying slowly about her decks. Such things had been known to happen.

Mr Burns met my outburst by a mysterious silence.

'Look here,' I said, 'you don't believe yourself what you say. You can't. It's impossible. It isn't the sort of thing I have a right to expect from you. My position's bad enough without being worried with your silly fancies.'

He remained unmoved. On account of the way in which the light fell on his head I could not be sure whether he had smiled faintly or not. I changed my tone.

'Listen,' I said. 'It's getting so desperate that I had thought for a moment, since we can't make our way south, whether I wouldn't try to steer west and make an attempt to reach the mail-boat track. We could always get some quinine from her, at least. What do you think?'

He cried out, 'No, no, no. Don't do that, sir. You mustn't for a moment give up facing that old ruffian. If you do he will get the upper hand of us.'

I left him. He was impossible. It was like a case of possession. His protest, however, was essentially quite sound. As a matter of fact, my notion of heading out west on the chance of sighting a problematical steamer could not bear calm examination. On the side where we were we had enough wind, at least from time to time, to struggle on towards the south – enough, at least, to keep hope alive. But suppose that I had used those capricious gusts of wind to sail away to the westward, into some region where there was not a breath of air for days on end, what then? Perhaps my appalling vision of a ship floating with a dead crew would become a reality for the discovery weeks afterwards by some horror-stricken mariners.

That afternoon Ransome brought me up a cup of tea, and while waiting there, tray in hand, he remarked in the exactly right tone of sympathy:

'You are holding out well, sir.'

'Yes,' I said. 'You and I seem to have been forgotten.'

'Forgotten, sir?'

'Yes, by the fever-devil who has got on board this ship,' I said.

Ransome gave me one of his attractive, intelligent, quick glances, and went away with the tray. It occurred to me that I had been talking somewhat in Mr Burns's manner. It annoyed me. Yet often in darker moments I forgot myself into an attitude towards our troubles more fit for a contest against a living enemy.

Yes. The fever-devil had not laid his hand yet either on Ransome or on me. But he might at any time. It was one of those thoughts one had to fight down, keep at arm's length at any cost. It was unbearable to contemplate the possibility of Ransome, the house-keeper of the ship, being laid low. And what would happen to my command if I got knocked over, with Mr Burns too weak to stand without holding on to his bed-place, and the second mate reduced to a state of permanent imbecility? It was impossible to imagine, or, rather, it was only too easy to imagine.

I was alone on the poop. The ship having no steerage way, I had sent the helmsman away to sit down or lie down somewhere in the shade. The men's strength was so reduced that all unnecessary calls on it had to be avoided. It was the austere Gambril with the grizzly beard. He went away readily enough, but he was so weakened by repeated bouts of fever, poor fellow, that in order to get down the poop ladder he had to turn sideways and hang on with both hands to the brass rail. It was just simply heartbreaking to watch. Yet he was neither very much worse nor much better than most of the half-dozen miserable victims I could muster up on deck.

It was a terribly lifeless afternoon. For several days in succes-sion low clouds had appeared in the distance, white masses with dark convolutions resting on the water, motionless, almost solid, and yet all the time changing their aspects subtly. Towards evening they vanished as a rule. But this day they awaited the setting sun, which glowed and smouldered sulkily amongst them before it sank down. The punctual and wearisome stars reap-peared over our mast-heads, but the air remained stagnant and oppressive.

The unfailing Ransome lighted the binnacle [7] lamps and glided, all shadowy, up to me.

'Will you go down and try to eat something, sir?' he suggested.

His low voice startled me. I had been standing looking out over the rail, saying nothing, feeling nothing, not even the weariness of my limbs, overcome by the evil spell.

'Ransome,' I asked abruptly, 'how long have I been on deck? I am losing the notion of time.'

'Fourteen days, sir,' he said. 'It was a fortnight last Monday since we left the anchorage.'

His equable voice sounded mournful somehow. He waited a bit, then added, 'It's the first time that it looks as if we were to have some rain.'

I noticed then the broad shadow on the horizon extinguishing the low stars completely, while those overhead, when I looked up, seemed to shine down on us through a veil of smoke.

How it got there, how it had crept up so high, I couldn't say. It had an ominous appearance. The air did not stir. At a renewed invitation from Ransome I did go down into the cabin to – in his words – 'try and eat something.' I don't know that the trial was very successful. I suppose at that period I did exist on food in the usual way; but the memory is now that in those days life was sustained on invincible anguish, as a sort of infernal stimulant exciting and consuming at the same time.

It's the only period of my life in which I attempted to keep a diary. No, not the only one. Years later, in conditions of moral isolation, I did put down on paper the thoughts and events of a score of days. But this was the first time. I don't remember how it came about, or how the pocket-book and the pencil came into my hands. It's inconceivable that I should have looked for them on purpose. I suppose they saved me from the crazy trick of talking to myself.

Strangely enough, in both cases I took to that sort of thing in circumstances in which I did not expect, in colloquial phrase, 'to come out of it.' Neither could I expect the record to outlast me. This shows that it was purely a personal need for intimate relief and not a call of egotism.

Here I must give another sample of it, a few detached lines, now looking very ghostly to my own eyes, out of the part scribbled that very evening:

'There is something going on in the sky like a decomposition, like a corruption of the air, which remains as still as ever. After all, mere clouds, which may or may not hold wind or rain. Strange that it should trouble me so. I feel as if all my sins had found me out. But I suppose the trouble is that the ship is still lying motionless, not under command; and that I have nothing to do to keep my imagination from running wild amongst the disastrous images of the worst that may befall us. What's going to happen? Probably nothing. Or anything. It may be a furious squall coming, butt-end foremost. And on deck there are five men with the vitality and the strength of, say, two. We may have all our sails blown away. Every stitch of canvas has been on her since we broke ground at the mouth of the Meinam,[8] fifteen days ago ... or fifteen centuries. It seems to me that all my life before that momentous day is infinitely remote, a fading memory of light-hearted youth, something on the other side of a shadow. Yes, sails may very well be blown away. And that would be like a death sentence on the men. We haven't strength enough on board to bend another suit;[9] incredible thought, but it is true. Or we may even get dismasted. Ships have been dismasted in squalls simply because they weren't handled quick enough, and we have no power to whirl the yards around. It's like being bound hand and foot preparatory to having one's throat cut. And what appals me most of all is that I shrink from going on deck to face it. It's due to the ship, it's due to the men who are there on deck – some of them ready to put out the last remnant of their strength at a word from me. And I am shrinking from it. From the mere vision. My first command. Now I understand that strange sense of insecurity in my past. I always suspected that I might be no good. And here is proof positive. I am shirking it. I am no good.'

At that moment, or, perhaps, the moment after, I became aware of Ransome standing in the cabin. Something in his expression startled me. It had a meaning which I could not make out. I exclaimed:

'Somebody's dead!'

It was his turn then to look startled.

'Dead? Not that I know of, sir. I have been in the forecastle only ten minutes ago, and there was no dead man there then.'

'You did give me a scare,' I said.

His voice was extremely pleasant to listen to. He explained that he had come down below to close Mr Burns's port in case it should come on to rain. He did not know that I was in the cabin, he added.

'How does it look outside?' I asked him.

'Very black indeed, sir. There is something in it for certain.'

'In what quarter?'

'All round, sir.'

I repeated idly, 'All round. For certain,' with my elbows on the table.

Ransome lingered in the cabin as if he had something to do there, but hesitated about doing it. I said suddenly:

'You think I ought to be on deck?'

He answered at once, but without any particular emphasis or accent, 'I do, sir.'

I got to my feet briskly, and he made way for me to go out. As I passed through the lobby I heard Mr Burns's voice saying:

'Shut the door of my room, will you, steward?'

And Ransome's rather surprised, 'Certainly, sir.'

I thought that all my feelings had been dulled into complete indifference. But I found it as trying as ever to be on deck. The impenetrable blackness beset the ship so close that it seemed that by thrusting one's hand over the side one could touch some unearthly substance. There was in it an effect of inconceivable terror and of inexpressible mystery. The few stars overhead shed a dim light upon the ship alone, with no gleams of any kind upon the water, in detached shafts piercing an atmosphere which had turned to soot. It was something I had never seen before, giving no hint of the direction from which any change would come, the closing in of a menace from all sides.

There was still no man at the helm. The immobility of all things was perfect. If the air had turned black, the sea, for all I knew, might have turned solid. It was no good looking in any direction, watching for any sign, speculating upon the nearness of the moment. When the time came the blackness would overwhelm silently the bit of starlight falling upon the ship, and the end of all things would come without a sigh, stir, or murmur of any kind, and all our hearts would cease to beat, like run-down clocks.

It was impossible to shake off that sense of finality. The quietness that came over me was like a foretaste of annihilation. It gave me a sort of comfort, as though my soul had become suddenly reconciled to an eternity of blind stillness.

The seaman's instinct alone survived whole in my moral dissolution. I descended the ladder to the quarter-deck. The starlight seemed to die out before reaching that spot, but when I asked quietly, 'Are you there, men?' my eyes made out shadowy forms starting up around me, very few, very indistinct; and a voice spoke, 'All here, sir.' Another amended anxiously:

'All that are good for anything, sir.'

Both voices were very quiet and unringing; without any special character of readiness or discouragement. Very matter-of-fact voices.

'We must try to haul this mainsail [10] close up.' I said.

The shadows swayed away from me without a word. Those men were the ghosts of themselves, and their weight on a rope could be no more than the weight of a bunch of ghosts. Indeed, if ever a sail was hauled up by sheer spiritual strength it must have been that sail, for, properly speaking, there was not muscle enough for the task in the whole ship, let alone the miserable lot of us on deck. Of course, I took the lead in the work myself. They wandered feebly after me from rope to rope, stumbling and panting. They toiled like Titans. We were an hour at it at least, and all the time the black universe made no sound. When the last leech-line [11] was made fast, my eyes, accustomed to the darkness, made out the shapes of exhausted men drooping over the rails, collapsed on hatches. One hung over the after-capstan, [12] sobbing for breath; and I stood amongst them like a tower of strength, impervious to disease, and feeling only the sickness of my soul. I waited for some time fighting against the weight of my sins, against my sense of unworthiness, and then I said:

'Now, men, we'll go aft and square the mainyard. [13] That's about all we can do for the ship; and for the rest she must take her chance.'

CHAPTER SIX

As we all went up it occurred to me that there ought to be a man at the helm. I raised my voice not much above a whisper, and, noiselessly, an uncomplaining spirit in a fever-wasted body appeared in the light aft, the head with hollow eyes illuminated against the blackness which had swallowed up our world – and the universe. The bared forearm extended over the upper spokes seemed to shine with a light of its own.

I murmured to that luminous appearance:

'Keep the helm right amidships.'[1]

It answered in a tone of patient suffering:

'Right amidships, sir.'

Then I descended to the quarter-deck. It was impossible to tell whence the blow would come. To look round the ship was to look into a bottomless, black pit. The eye lost itself in inconceivable depths.

I wanted to ascertain whether the ropes had been picked up off the deck. One could only do that by feeling with one's feet. In my cautious progress I came against a man in whom I recognised Ransome. He possessed an unimpaired physical solidity which was manifest to me at the contact. He was leaning against the quarter-deck capstan and kept silent. It was like a revelation. He was the collapsed figure sobbing for breath I had noticed before we went on the poop.

'You have been helping with the mainsail!' I exclaimed in a low tone.

'Yes, sir,' sounded his quiet voice.

'Man! What were you thinking of? You mustn't do that sort of thing.'

After a pause he assented. 'I suppose I mustn't.' Then after another short silence he added, 'I am all right now,' quickly, between the tell-tale gasps.

I could neither hear nor see anybody else; but when I spoke up, answering sad murmurs filled the quarter-deck, and its shadows seemed to shift here and there. I ordered all the halyards [2] laid down on deck clear for running. [3]

'I'll see to that, sir,' volunteered Ransome in his natural, pleasant tone, which comforted one and aroused one's compassion too, somehow.

That man ought to have been in his bed, resting, and my plain duty was to send him there. But perhaps he would not have obeyed me. I had not the strength of mind to try. All I said was:

'Go about it quietly, Ransome.'

Returning on the poop I approached Gambril. His face, set with hollow shadows in the light, looked awful, finally silenced. I asked him how he felt, but hardly expected an answer. Therefore I was astonished at his comparative loquacity.

'Them shakes leaves me as weak as a kitten, sir,' he said, preserving finely that air of unconsciousness as to anything but his business a helmsman should never lose. 'And before I can pick up my strength that there hot fit comes along and knocks me over again.'

He sighed. There was no complaint in his tone, but the bare words were enough to give me a horrible pang of self-reproach. It held me dumb for a time. When the tormenting sensation had passed off I asked:

'Do you feel strong enough to prevent the rudder taking charge if she gets sternway [4] on her? It wouldn't do to get something smashed about the steering-gear now. We've enough difficulties to cope with as it is.'

He answered with just a shade of weariness that he was strong enough to hang on. He could promise me that she shouldn't take the wheel out of his hands. More he couldn't say.

At that moment Ransome appeared quite close to me, stepping out of the darkness into visibility suddenly, as if just created with his composed face and pleasant voice.

Every rope on deck, he said, was laid down clear for running, as far as one could make certain by feeling. It was impossible to see anything. Frenchy had stationed himself forward. He said he had a jump or two left in him yet.

Here a faint smile altered for an instant the clear, firm design of

Ransome's lips. With his serious, clear grey eyes, his serene temperament, he was a priceless man altogether. Soul as firm as the muscles of his body.

He was the only man on board (except me, but I had to preserve my liberty of movement) who had a sufficiency of muscular strength to trust to. For a moment I thought I had better ask him to take the wheel. But the dreadful knowledge of the enemy he had to carry about him made me hesitate. In my ignorance of physiology it occurred to me that he might die suddenly, from excitement, at a critical moment.

While this gruesome fear restrained the ready words on the tip of my tongue, Ransome stepped back two paces and vanished from my sight.

At once an uneasiness possessed me, as if some support had been withdrawn. I moved forward too, outside the circle of light, into the darkness that stood in front of me like a wall. In one stride I penetrated it. Such must have been the darkness before creation. It had closed behind me. I knew I was invisible to the man at the helm. Neither could I see anything. He was alone, I was alone, every man was alone where he stood. And every form was gone too, spar, sail, fittings, rails; everything was blotted out in the dreadful smoothness of that absolute night.

A flash of lightning would have been a relief – I mean physically. I would have prayed for it if it hadn't been for my shrinking apprehension of the thunder. In the tension of silence I was suffering from it seemed to me that the first crash must turn me into dust.

And thunder was, most likely, what would happen next. Stiff all over and hardly breathing, I waited with a horribly strained expectation. Nothing happened. It was maddening. But a dull, growing ache in the lower part of my face made me aware that I had been grinding my teeth madly enough, for God knows how long.

It's extraordinary I should not have heard myself doing it; but I hadn't. By an effort which absorbed all my faculties I managed to keep my jaw still. It required much attention, and while thus engaged I became bothered by curious, irregular sounds of faint tapping on the deck. They could be heard single, in pairs, in groups.

While I wondered at this mysterious devilry, I received a slight blow under the left eye and felt an enormous tear run down my cheek. Raindrops. Enormous. Forerunners of something. Tap, tap, tap . . .

I turned about, and, addressing Gambril earnestly, entreated him to 'hang on to the wheel.' But I could hardly speak from emotion. The fatal moment had come. I held my breath. The tapping had stopped as unexpectedly as it had begun, and there was a renewed moment of intolerable suspense; something like an additional turn of the racking screw. I don't suppose I would have ever screamed, but I remember my conviction that there was nothing else for it but to scream.

Suddenly – how am I to convey it? Well, suddenly the darkness turned into water. This is the only suitable figure. A heavy shower, a downpour, comes along, making a noise. You hear its approach on the sea, in the air too, I verily believe. But this was different. With no preliminary whisper or rustle, without a splash, and even without the ghost of impact, I became instantaneously soaked to the skin. Not a very difficult matter, since I was wearing only my sleeping-suit. My hair got full of water in an instant, water streamed on my skin, it filled my nose, my ears, my eyes. In a fraction of a second I swallowed quite a lot of it.

As to Gambril, he was fairly choked. He coughed pitifully, the broken cough of a sick man; and I beheld him as one sees a fish in an aquarium by the light of an electric bulb, an elusive, phosphorescent shape. Only he did not glide away. But something else happened. Both binnacle lamps went out. I suppose the water forced itself into them, though I wouldn't have thought that possible, for they fitted into the cowl perfectly.

The last gleam of light in the universe had gone, pursued by a low exclamation of dismay from Gambril. I groped for him and seized his arm. How startlingly wasted it was.

'Never mind,' I said. 'You don't want the light. All you need to do is to keep the wind, when it comes, at the back of your head. You understand?'

'Aye, aye, sir . . . But I should like to have a light,' he added nervously.

All that time the ship lay as steady as a rock. The noise of the water pouring off the sails and spars, flowing over the break of the poop,[5] had stopped short. The poop scuppers[6] gurgled and sobbed for a little while longer, and then perfect silence, joined to perfect immobility, proclaimed the yet unbroken spell of our helplessness, poised on the edge of some violent issue, lurking in the dark.

I started forward restlessly. I did not need my sight to pace the poop of my ill-starred first command with perfect assurance. Every square foot of her decks was impressed indelibly on my brain, to the very grain and knots of the planks. Yet, all of a sudden, I fell clean over something, landing full length on my hands and face.

It was something big and alive. Not a dog – more like a sheep, rather. But there were no animals in the ship. How could an animal . . . It was an added and fantastic horror which I could not resist. The hair of my head stirred even as I picked myself up, awfully scared; not as a man is scared while his judgment, his reason still try to resist, but completely, boundlessly, and, as it were, innocently scared – like a little child.

I could see It – that Thing! The darkness, of which so much had just turned into water, had thinned down a little. There It was! But I did not hit upon the notion of Mr Burns issuing out of the companion on all fours till he attempted to stand up, and even then the idea of a bear crossed my mind first.

He growled like one when I seized him round the body. He had buttoned himself up into an enormous winter overcoat of some woolly material, the weight of which was too much for his reduced state. I could hardly feel the incredibly thin lath of his body, lost within the thick stuff, but his growl had depth and substance: Confounded dumb ship with a craven, tiptoeing crowd. Why couldn't they stamp and go with a brace? Wasn't there one God-forsaken lubber[7] in the lot fit to raise a yell on a rope?

'Skulking's no good, sir,' he attacked me directly. 'You can't slink past the old murderous ruffian. It isn't the way. You must go for him boldly – as I did. Boldness is what you want. Show him that you don't care for any of his damned tricks. Kick up a jolly old row.'

'Good God, Mr Burns!' I said angrily. 'What on earth are you up to? What do you mean by coming up on deck in this state?'

'Just that! Boldness. The only way to scare the old bullying rascal.'

I pushed him, still growling, against the rail. 'Hold on to it,' I said roughly. I did not know what to do with him. I left him in a hurry, to go to Gambril, who had called faintly that he believed there was some wind aloft. Indeed, my own ears had caught a feeble flutter of wet canvas, high up overhead, the jingle of a slack chain sheet . . .[8]

These were eerie, disturbing, alarming sounds in the dead stillness of the air around me. All the instances I had heard of topmasts being whipped out of a ship while there was not wind enough on her deck to blow out a match rushed into my memory.

'I can't see the upper sails, sir,' declared Gambril shakily.

'Don't move the helm. You'll be all right,' I said confidently.

The poor man's nerve was gone. I was not in much better case. It was the moment of breaking strain and was relieved by the abrupt sensation of the ship moving forward as if of herself under my feet. I heard plainly the soughing of the wind aloft, the low cracks of the upper spars taking the strain, long before I could feel the least draught on my face turned aft, anxious and sightless like the face of a blind man.

Suddenly a louder sounding note filled our ears, the darkness started streaming against our bodies, chilling them exceedingly. Both of us, Gambril and I, shivered violently in our clinging, soaked garments of thin cotton. I said to him:

'You are all right now, my man. All you've got to do is to keep the wind at the back of your head. Surely you are up to that. A child could steer this ship in smooth water.'

He muttered, 'Aye! A healthy child.' And I felt ashamed of having been passed over by the fever which had been preying on every man's strength but mine, in order that my remorse might be the more bitter, the feeling of unworthiness more poignant, and the sense of responsibility heavier to bear.

The ship had gathered great way on her almost at once on the calm water. I felt her slipping through it with no other noise but a mysterious rustle alongside. Otherwise she had no motion at all, neither lift nor roll. It was a disheartening steadiness which had lasted for eighteen days now; for never, never had we had wind enough in that time to raise the slightest run of the sea.[9] The breeze freshened suddenly. I thought it was high time to get Mr Burns off the deck. He worried me. I looked upon him as a lunatic who would be very likely to start roaming over the ship and break a limb or fall overboard.

I was truly glad to find he had remained holding on where I had left him, sensibly enough. He was, however, muttering to himself ominously.

This was discouraging. I remarked in a matter-of-fact tone:

'We have never had so much wind as this since we left the roads.' [10]

'There's some heart in it too,' he growled judiciously. It was a remark of a perfectly sane seaman. But he added immediately, 'It was about time I should come on deck. I've been nursing my strength for this – just for this. Do you see it, sir?'

I said I did, and proceeded to hint that it would be advisable for him to go below now and take a rest.

His answer was an indignant, 'Go below! Not if I know it, sir.'

Very cheerful! He was a horrible nuisance. And all at once he started to argue. I could feel his crazy excitement in the dark.

'You don't know how to go about it, sir. How could you? All this whispering and tiptoeing is no good. You can't hope to slink past a cunning, wide-awake, evil brute like he was. You never heard him talk. Enough to make your hair stand on end. No, no! He wasn't mad. He was no more mad than I am. He was just downright wicked. Wicked so as to frighten most people. I will tell you what he was. He was nothing less than a thief and a murderer at heart. And do you think he's any different now because he's dead? Not he! His carcass lies a hundred fathom under, but he's just the same . . . in latitude 8° 20′ North.'

He snorted defiantly. I noted with weary resignation that the breeze had got lighter while he raved. He was at it again.

'I ought to have thrown the beggar out of the ship over the rail like a dog. It was only on account of the men . . . Fancy having to read the Burial Service over a brute like that! . . . "Our departed brother" . . . I could have laughed. That was what he couldn't bear. I suppose I am the only man that ever stood up to laugh at him. When he got sick it used to scare that . . . brother . . . Brother . . . Departed . . . Sooner call a shark brother.'

The breeze had let go so suddenly that the way of the ship brought the wet sails heavily against the masts. The spell of deadly stillness had caught us up again. There seemed to be no escape.

'Hullo!' exclaimed Mr Burns in a startled voice. 'Calm again!'

I addressed him as though he had been sane.

'This is the sort of thing we've been having for seventeen days, Mr Burns,' I said, with intense bitterness. 'A puff, then a calm, and in a moment, you'll see, she'll be swinging on her heel with her head away from her course to the devil somewhere.'

He caught at the word. 'The old dodging devil!' he screamed piercingly, and burst into such a loud laugh as I had never heard before. It was a provoking, mocking peal, with a hair-raising, screeching over-note of defiance. I stepped back utterly confounded.

Instantly there was a stir in the quarter-deck, murmurs of dismay. A distressed voice cried out in the dark below us, 'Who's that gone crazy, now?'

Perhaps they thought it was their captain! Rush is not the word that could be applied to the utmost speed the poor fellows were up to; but in an amazingly short time every man in the ship able to walk upright had found his way on to that poop.

I shouted at them, 'It's the mate. Lay hold of him, a couple of you . . .'

I expected this performance to end in a ghastly sort of fight. But Mr Burns cut his derisive screeching dead short and turned upon them fiercely, yelling:

'Aha! Dog-gone ye! You've found your tongues – have ye? I thought you were dumb. Well, then – laugh! Laugh – I tell you. Now then – all together. One, two, three – laugh!'

A moment of silence ensued, of silence so profound that you could have heard a pin drop on the deck. Then Ransome's unperturbed voice uttered pleasantly the words:

'I think he has fainted, sir –' The little motionless knot of men stirred, with low murmurs of relief. 'I've got him under the arms. Get hold of his legs, some one.'

Yes. It was a relief. He was silenced for a time – for a time. I could not have stood another peal of that insane screeching. I was sure of it; and just then Gambril, the austere Gambril, treated us to another vocal performance. He began to sing out for relief. His voice wailed pitifully in the darkness. 'Come aft, somebody! I can't stand this. Here she'll be off again directly and I can't . . .'

I dashed aft myself, meeting on my way a hard gust of wind whose approach Gambril's ear had detected from afar and which filled the sails on the main in a series of muffled reports mingled with the low plaint of the spars. I was just in time to seize the wheel while Frenchy, who had followed me, caught up the collapsing Gambril. He hauled him out of the way, admonished him to lie still where he was, and then stepped up to relieve me, asking calmly:

'How am I to steer her, sir?'

'Dead before it, for the present. I'll get you a light in a moment.'

But going forward I met Ransome bringing up the spare binnacle lamp. That man noticed everything, attended to everything, shed comfort around him as he moved. As he passed me he remarked in a soothing tone that the stars were coming out. They were. The breeze was sweeping clear the sooty sky, breaking through the indolent silence of the sea.

The barrier of awful stillness which had encompassed us for so many days as though we had been accursed was broken. I felt that. I let myself fall on to the skylight seat. A faint white ridge of foam, thin, very thin, broke alongside. The first for ages – for ages. I could have cheered, if it hadn't been for the sense of guilt which clung to all my thoughts secretly. Ransome stood before me.

'What about the mate?' I asked anxiously. 'Still unconscious?'

'Well, sir – it's funny.' Ransome was evidently puzzled. 'He hasn't spoken a word, and his eyes are shut. But it looks to me more like sound sleep than anything else.'

I accepted this view as the least troublesome of any, or, at any rate, least disturbing. Dead faint or deep slumber, Mr Burns had to be left to himself for the present. Ransome remarked suddenly:

'I believe you want a coat, sir.'

'I believe I do,' I sighed out.

But I did not move. What I felt I wanted were new limbs. My ams and legs seemed utterly useless, fairly worn out. They didn't even ache. But I stood up all the same to put on the coat when

Ransome brought it up. And when he suggested that he had better now 'take Gambril forward,' I said:

'All right. I'll help you get him down on the main-deck.'

I found that I was quite able to help, too. We raised Gambril up between us. He tried to help himself along like a man, but all the time he was inquiring piteously:

'You won't let me go when we come to the ladder? You won't let me go when we come to the ladder?'

The breeze kept on freshening and blew true, true to a hair. At daylight by careful manipulation of the helm we got the foreyards to run square by themselves (the water keeping smooth) and then went about hauling the ropes tight. Of the four men I had with me at night, I could see now only two. I didn't inquire as to the others. They had given in. For a time only, I hoped.

Our various tasks forward occupied us for hours, the two men with me moved so slowly and had to rest so often. One of them remarked that 'every blamed thing in the ship felt about a hundred times heavier than its proper weight.' This was the only complaint uttered. I don't know what we should have done without Ransome. He worked with us, silent too, with a little smile frozen on his lips. From time to time I murmured to him, 'Go steady' – 'Take it easy, Ransome' – and received a quick glance in reply.

When we had done all we could do to make things safe, he disappeared into his galley. Some time afterwards, going forward for a look round, I caught sight of him through the open door. He sat upright on the locker in front of the stove, with his head leaning back against the bulkhead. His eyes were closed; his capable hands held open the front of his thin cotton shirt, baring tragically his powerful chest, which heaved in painful and laboured gasps. He didn't hear me.

I retreated quietly and went straight on to the poop to relieve Frenchy, who by that time was beginning to look very sick. He gave me the course with great formality and tried to go off with a jaunty step, but reeled widely twice before getting out of my sight.

And then I remained all alone aft, steering my ship, which ran before the wind with a buoyant lift now and then, and even rolling a little. Presently Ransome appeared before me with a tray. The sight of food made me ravenous all at once. He took the wheel while I sat down on the after-grating[11] to eat my breakfast.

'This breeze seems to have done for our crowd,' he murmured. 'It just laid them low – all hands.'

'Yes,' I said. 'I suppose you and I are the only two fit men in the ship.'

'Frenchy says there's still a jump left in him. I don't know. It can't be much,' continued Ransome, with his wistful smile. 'Good little man that. But suppose, sir, that this wind flies round when we are close to the land – what are we going to do with her?'

'If the wind shifts round heavily after we close in with the land she will either run ashore or get dismasted or both. We won't be able to do anything with her. She's running away with us now. All we can do is to steer her. She's a ship without a crew.'

'Yes. All laid low,' repeated Ransome quietly. 'I do give them a look-in forward every now and then, but it's precious little I can do for them.'

'I, and the ship, and every one on board of her, are very much indebted to you, Ransome,' I said warmly.

He made as though he had not heard me, and steered in silence till I was ready to relieve him. He surrendered the wheel, picked up the tray, and for a parting shot informed me that Mr Burns was awake and seemed to have a mind to come up on deck.

'I don't know how to prevent him, sir. I can't very well stop down below all the time.'

It was clear that he couldn't. And sure enough Mr Burns came on deck dragging himself painfully aft in his enormous overcoat. I beheld him with a natural dread. To have him around and raving about the wiles of a dead man while I had to steer a wildly rushing ship full of dying men was a rather dreadful prospect.

But his first remarks were quite sensible in meaning and tone. Apparently he had no recollection of the night scene. And if he had he didn't betray himself once. Neither did he talk very much. He sat on the skylight looking desperately ill at first, but that strong breeze, before which the last remnant of my crew had wilted down, seemed to blow a fresh stock of vigour into his frame with every gust. One could almost see the process.

By way of sanity test I alluded on purpose to the late captain. I was delighted to find that Mr Burns did not display undue interest in the subject. He ran over the old tale of that savage ruffian's iniquities with a certain vindictive gusto and then concluded unexpectedly:

'I do believe, sir, that his brain began to go a year or more before he died.'

A wonderful recovery. I could hardly spare it as much admiration as it deserved, for I had to give all my mind to the steering.

In comparison with the hopeless languor of the preceding days this was dizzy speed. Two ridges of foam streamed from the ship's bows; the wind sang in a strenuous note which under other circumstances would have expressed to me all the joy of life. Whenever the hauled-up mainsail started trying to slat[12] and bang itself to pieces in its gear, Mr Burns would look at me apprehensively.

'What would you have me do, Mr Burns? We can neither furl it nor set it. I only wish the old thing would thrash itself to pieces and be done with it. This beastly racket confuses me.'

Mr Burns wrung his hands, and cried out suddenly:

'How will the ship get into harbour, sir, without men to handle her?'

And I couldn't tell him.

Well – it did get done about forty hours afterwards. By the exorcising virtue of Mr Burns's awful laugh, the malicious spectre had been laid, the evil spell broken, the curse removed. We were now in the hands of a kind and energetic Providence. It was rushing us on . . .

I shall never forget the last night, dark, windy, and starry. I steered. Mr Burns, after having obtained from me a solemn promise to give him a kick if anything happened, went frankly to sleep on the deck close to the binnacle. Convalescents need sleep. Ransome, his back propped against the mizzenmast[13] and a blanket over his legs, remained perfectly still, but I don't suppose he closed his eyes for a moment. That embodiment of jauntiness, Frenchy, still under the delusion that there was 'a jump' left in him, had insisted on joining us; but, mindful of discipline, had laid himself down as far on the forepart of the poop as he could get, alongside the bucket-rack.

And I steered, too tired for anxiety, too tired for connected thought. I had moments of grim exultation and then my heart would sink awfully at the thought of that forecastle at the other end of the dark deck, full of fever-stricken men – some of them dying. By my fault. But never mind. Remorse must wait. I had to steer.

In the small hours the breeze weakened, then failed altogether. About five it returned, gentle enough, enabling us to head for the roadstead. Daybreak found Mr Burns sitting wedged up with coils of rope on the stern-grating, and from the depths of his overcoat steering the ship with very white, bony hands; while Ransome and I rushed along the decks letting go all the sheets and halyards by the run. We dashed next up on to the forecastle head. The perspiration of labour and sheer nervousness simply poured off our heads as we toiled to get the anchors cock-billed.[14] I dared not look at Ransome as we worked side by side. We exchanged curt words; I could hear him panting close to me and I avoided turning my eyes his way for fear of seeing him fall down and expire in the act of putting out his strength – for what? Indeed, for some distinct ideal.

The consummate seaman in him was aroused. He needed no directions. He knew what to do. Every effort, every movement was an act of consistent heroism. It was not for me to look at a man thus inspired.

At last all was ready, and I heard him say, 'Hadn't I better go down and open the compressors[15] now, sir?'

'Yes. Do,' I said. And even then I did not glance his way. After a time his voice came up from the main-deck:

'When you like, sir. All clear on the windlass here.'

I made a sign to Mr Burns to put the helm down, and then I let both anchors go one after another, leaving the ship to take as much cable as she wanted. She took the best part of them both before she brought up. The loose sails coming aback ceased their maddening racket above my head. A perfect stillness reigned in the ship. And while I stood forward feeling a little giddy in that sudden peace, I caught faintly a moan or two and the incoherent mutterings of the sick in the forecastle.

As we had a signal for medical assistance flying on the mizzen it is a fact that before the ship was fairly at rest three steam-launches from various men-of-war[16] arrived alongside; and at least five naval surgeons[17] clambered on board. They stood in a knot gazing up and down the empty main-deck, then looked aloft – where not a man could be seen either.

I went towards them – a solitary figure in a blue-and-grey striped sleeping-suit and a pipeclayed cork helmet on its head. Their disgust was extreme. They had expected surgical cases. Each one had brought his carving tools with him. But they soon got over their little disappointment. In less than five minutes one of the steam-launches was rushing shorewards to order a big boat and some hospital people for the removal of the crew. The big steam-pinnace[18] went off to her ship to bring over a few bluejackets[19] to furl my sails for me.

One of the surgeons had remained on board. He came out of the forecastle looking impenetrable, and noticed my inquiring gaze.

'There's nobody dead in there, if that's what you want to know,' he said deliberately. Then added in a tone of wonder, 'The whole crew!'

'And very bad?'

'And very bad,' he repeated. His eyes were roaming all over the ship. 'Heavens! What's that?'

'That,' I said, glancing aft, 'is Mr Burns, my chief officer.'

Mr Burns, with his moribund head nodding on the stalk of his lean neck, was a sight for any one to exclaim at. The surgeon asked:

'Is he going to the hospital too?'

'Oh no,' I said jocosely. 'Mr Burns can't go on shore till the mainmast goes. I am very proud of him. He's my only convalescent.'

'You look . . .' began the doctor, staring at me. But I interrupted him angrily:

'I am not ill.'

'No . . . You look queer.'

'Well, you see, I have been seventeen days on deck.'

'Seventeen! . . . But you must have slept.'

'I suppose I must have. I don't know. But I'm certain that I didn't sleep for the last forty hours.'

'Phew! . . . You will be going ashore presently, I suppose?'

As soon as ever I can. There's no end of business waiting for me there.'

The surgeon released my hand, which he had taken while we talked, pulled out his pocket-book, wrote in it rapidly, tore out the page, and offered it to me.

'I strongly advise you to get this prescription made up for yourself ashore. Unless I am much mistaken you will need it this evening.'

'What is it then?' I asked, with suspicion.

'Sleeping draught,' answered the surgeon curtly; and moving with an air of interest towards Mr Burns he engaged him in conversation.

As I went below to dress to go ashore, Ransome followed me. He begged my pardon; he wished, too, to be sent ashore and paid off.

I looked at him in surprise. He was waiting for my answer with an air of anxiety.

'You don't mean to leave the ship!' I cried out.

'I do really, sir. I want to go and be quiet somewhere. Anywhere. The hospital will do.'

'But, Ransome,' I said, 'I hate the idea of parting with you.'

'I must go,' he broke in. 'I have a right!' He gasped, and a look of almost savage determination passed over his face. For an instant he was another being. And I saw under the worth and the comeliness of the man the humble reality of things. Life was a boon to him – this precarious hard life – and he was thoroughly alarmed about himself.

'Of course I shall pay you off if you wish it,' I hastened to say. 'Only I must ask you to remain on board till this afternoon. I can't leave Mr Burns absolutely by himself in the ship for hours.'

He softened at once and assured me with a smile and in his natural pleasant voice that he understood that very well.

When I returned on deck everything was ready for the removal of the men. It was the last ordeal of that episode which had been maturing and tempering my character – though I did not know it.

It was awful. They passed under my eyes one after another – each of them an embodied reproach of the bitterest kind, till I felt a sort of revolt wake up in me. Poor Frenchy had gone suddenly under. He was carried past me insensible, his comic face horribly flushed and as if swollen, breathing stertorously. He looked more like Mr Punch than ever; a disgracefully intoxicated Mr Punch.

The austere Gambril, on the contrary, had improved temporarily. He insisted on walking on his own feet to the rail – of course with assistance on each side of him. But he gave way to a sudden panic at the moment of being swung over the side and began to wail pitifully:

'Don't let them drop me, sir. Don't let them drop me, sir!' While I kept on shouting to him in most soothing accents, 'All right, Gambril. They won't! They wont'!'

It was no doubt very ridiculous. The bluejackets on our deck were grinning quietly, while even Ransome himself (much to the fore in lending a hand) had to enlarge his wistful smile for a fleeting moment.

I left for the shore in the steam-pinnace, and on looking back beheld Mr Burns actually standing up by the taffrail, still in his enormous woolly overcoat. The bright sunlight brought out his weirdness amazingly. He looked like a frightful and elaborate scarecrow set up on the poop of a death-stricken ship, to keep the sea-birds from the corpses.

Our story had got about already in town and everybody on shore was most kind. The Marine Office let me off the port dues,[20] and as there happened to be a shipwrecked crew[21] staying in the Home I had no difficulty in obtaining as many men as I wanted. But when I inquired if I could see Captain Ellis for a moment, I was told in accents of pity for my ignorance that our deputy-Neptune had retired and gone home on a pension about three weeks after I left the port. So I suppose that my appointment was the last act outside the daily routine, of his official life.

It is strange how on coming ashore I was struck by the springy step, the lively eyes, the strong vitality of every one I met. It impressed me enormously. And amongst those I met there was Captain Giles, of course. It would have been very extraordinary if I had not met him. A prolonged stroll in the business part of the town was the regular employment of all his mornings when he was ashore.

I caught the glitter of the gold watch-chain across his chest ever so far away. He radiated benevolence.

'What is it I hear?' he queried, with a 'kind uncle' smile, after shaking hands. 'Twenty-one days from Bangkok?'

'Is this all you've heard?' I said. 'You must come to tiffin with me. I want you to know exactly what you have let me in for.'

He hesitated for almost a minute.

'Well – I will,' he decided condescendingly at last.

We turned into the hotel. I found to my surprise that I could eat quite a lot. Then over the cleared tablecloth I unfolded to Captain Giles all the story since I took command in all its professional and emotional aspects, while he smoked patiently the big cigar I had given him.

Then he observed sagely:

'You must feel jolly well tired by this time.'

'No,' I said. 'Not tired. But I'll tell you, Captain Giles, how I feel. I feel old. And I must be. All of you on shore look to me just a lot of skittish youngsters that have never known a care in the world.'

He didn't smile. He looked insufferably exemplary. He declared:

'That will pass. But you do look older – it's a fact.'

'Aha!' I said.

'No, no! The truth is that one must not make too much of anything in life, good or bad.'

'Live at half-speed,' I murmured perversely. 'Not everybody can do that.'

'You'll be glad enough presently if you can keep going even at that rate,' he retorted, with his air of conscious virtue. 'And there's another thing: a man should stand up to his bad luck, to his mistakes, to his conscience, and all that sort of thing. Why – what else would you have to fight against?'

I kept silent. I don't know what he saw in my face, but he asked abruptly:

'Why – you aren't faint-hearted?'

'God only knows, Captain Giles,' was my sincere answer.

'That's all right,' he said calmly. 'You will learn soon how not to be faint-hearted. A man has got to learn everything – and that's what so many of those youngsters don't understand.'

'Well, I am no longer a youngster.'

'No,' he conceded. 'Are you leaving soon?'

'I am going on board directly,' I said. 'I shall pick up one of my anchors and heave in to half-cable on the other as soon as my new crew comes on board, and I shall be off at daylight to-morrow.'[22]

'You will?' grunted Captain Giles approvingly. 'That's the way. You'll do.'

'What did you expect? That I would want to take a week ashore for a rest?' I said, irritated by his tone. 'There's no rest for me till she's out in the Indian Ocean, and not much of it even then.'

He puffed at the cigar moodily, as if transformed.

'Yes, that's what it amounts to,' he said in a musing tone. It was as if a ponderous curtain had rolled up, disclosing an unexpected Captain Giles. But it was only for a moment, merely the time to let him add, 'Precious little rest in life for anybody. Better not think of it.'

We rose, left the hotel, and parted from each other in the street with a warm handshake, just as he began to interest me for the first time in our intercourse.

The first thing I saw when I got back to the ship was Ransome on the quarter-deck sitting quietly on his neatly lashed sea-chest.

I beckoned him to follow me into the saloon, where I sat down to write a letter of recommendation for him to a man I knew on shore.

When finished, I pushed it across the table. 'It may be of some good to you when you leave the hospital.'

He took it, put it in his pocket. His eyes were looking away from me – nowhere. His face was anxiously set.

'How are you feeling now?' I asked.

'I don't feel bad now, sir,' he answered stiffly. 'But I am afraid of its coming on . . .' The wistful smile came back on his lips for a moment. 'I – I am in a blue funk about my heart, sir.'

I approached him with extended hand. His eyes, not looking at me, had a strained expression. He was like a man listening for a warning call.

'Won't you shake hands, Ransome?' I said gently.

He exclaimed, flushed up dusky red, gave my hand a hard wrench – and next moment, left alone in the cabin, I listened to him going up the companion stairs cautiously, step by step, in mortal fear of starting into sudden anger our common enemy it was his hard fate to carry consciously within his faithful breast.

EXPLANATORY NOTES

Given the drift of my argument in the Introduction, I have allowed these notes to tell the parallel story, in so far as it can be reconstructed, of Conrad's first command in early 1888. I have made liberal use of the findings of Conrad's three reliable modern biographers, viz. Jocelyn Baines, *Joseph Conrad: a Critical Biography*. Penguin Books, Harmondsworth, Middlesex (1960); Zdzisław Najder, *Joseph Conrad: A Chronicle*. Cambridge University Press (1983); and Norman Sherry, *Conrad's Eastern World*, Cambridge University Press (1966). In the following notes, I refer to these as Baines, Najder and Sherry, respectively. How the material they assemble is to be judged, in relation to Conrad's autobiographical claims, is a matter of perspective. To the historian, for whom factual error is a crime, it will undermine confidence in Conrad's veracity. To the critic, accustomed to the transformations of fiction, it will underscore how slight Conrad's deviations are from the original events, and how much of his life he has been able to admit into his narrative.

AUTHOR'S NOTE

1. *the origins of the feeling ... my mind* (p. 40). For 'the origins of the feeling', see the Introduction to this edition. As for the chronology, Conrad first thought of the story under the title *First Command* in 1899 (letter to William Blackwood, 14 February 1899); by early 1915 the writing was under way (letter to James Pinker, 3 February 1915); in October, renamed *The Shadow-Line*, it was at most half complete (letter to W. Rothenstein, 26 October 1915); it was finally finished on 17 December (letter to Richard Curle, 18 December).

2. *the year 1916* (p. 40). A mistake for 1915: Conrad told Curle that it was only in the last part of 1915 that he had been able to work hard at it. Edward Said has persuaded himself that this was some sort of Freudian slip, caused by Conrad's unconscious identification of the writing of the novel with his reading of Hartley Wither's *War and Lombard Street*, a discussion of the contribution of the banks to the war effort.

3. *As to locality . . . the greatest number of suggestions* (p. 40). Specifically, in terms of publication dates: *Almayer's Folly* (1895), *An Outcast of the Islands* (1896), 'Karain', 'The Lagoon' (1898), *Lord Jim* (1900), 'Youth', 'The End of the Tether' (1902), 'Typhoon', 'Falk' (1903), *'Twixt Land and Sea* (1912), 'The Planter of Malata', *Victory* (1915) and, after the *The Shadow-Line, The Rescue* (1920).

4. *the letter the owners of the ship wrote to me* (p. 41). This letter has survived. Dated Port Adelaide, 2 April 1889, it reads: 'Dear Sir, Referring to your resignation of the command (which we have in another letter formally accepted) of our bark *Otago*, we now have much pleasure in stating that this early severance from our employ is entirely at your own desire, with a view to visiting Europe, and that we entertain a high opinion of your ability in the capacity you now vacate, of your attainments generally, and should be glad to learn of your future success. Wishing you a pleasant passage home, We are, dear Sir, Yours faithfully, Henry Simpson & Sons, Owners of the Black Diamond Line' (G. Jean-Aubry, *Joseph Conrad, Life and Letters*, Heinemann, London (1927), Vol. I, p. 116).

5. *another portion of my writings* (p. 41). 'Heart of Darkness' (1902), and perhaps portions of *Chance* (1913).

CHAPTER ONE

1. *D'autres fois . . . mon désespoir* (p. 43). From Baudelaire's 'La Musique', in *Les Fleurs du Mal* ('Spleen et Idéal', LXIX). This is an irregular sonnet which can be rendered literally thus: 'Music often takes me like a sea! / Towards my pale star, / Under a ceiling of mist or in a vast ether, / I set sail; / With chest thrust forward and lungs inflated / Like canvas, / I scale the back of the heaped-up seas / That night veils from me; / I feel vibrating in me all the passions / Of a vessel that suffers; / The fair wind, the tempest and its convulsions / On the immense abyss/ Rock me. At other times, flat calm, great mirror / Of my despair!'

2. *It was in an Eastern port* (p. 44). Singapore (from the Malay 'Singapura': 'city of the lion'). Situated on an island at the southern tip of the Malay peninsula, it was conquered by Sir Stamford Raffles and ceded to the East India Company in 1819, and incorporated in the Straits Settlements Colony in 1826. Conrad knew it as a key trading port and naval fortress equidistant from India, China and the Archipelago.

3. *She was an Eastern ship* (p. 44). Conrad signed off the *Vidar* on 4 January 1888. This was a 204-ton steamer sailing regularly to and

from Borneo and Celebes, with a crew including four whites (the captain, the mate, two mechanics), one Chinese stoker, and twelve Malay sailors.

4. *the Red Ensign* (p. 44). The flag of the British Merchant Marine.

5. *taffrail* (p. 44). The rail round the edge of the aftermost part of the main deck.

6. *a house-flag ... white crescent* (p. 44). Red because of its association with the Merchant Service, green because of the colour of the flag of Saudi Arabia, and with a white crescent because of Islam.

7. *an Arab owned her, and a Syed at that* (p. 44). The owner of the *Vidar* was the respected and venerable Syed Moshin Bin Salleh Al Joffree. When Conrad met him, his fortunes were declining and his eyesight was failing. He died in 1894 aged eighty. 'Syed' is a title derived from the Arab word for 'lord', denoting 'a male descendant of Fatimah, daughter of Mohammed' (Sherry, p. 206).

8. *The charitable man is the friend of Allah* (p. 44). In the Koran, the Arabic name for the prophet Abraham (Alkhalil) means 'the friend of God', a title denoting his charitableness. Mohammed's immediate successor, the Calif Abubakr, is known to this day as Alkhalil because he relinquished all his worldly possessions.

9. *Kalashes* (p. 45). A word derived from the Malay noun *kelasi*, meaning 'sailor'; cf. *Youth* (Dent Collected Edition), p. 27: 'Four Calashes pulled a swinging stroke. This was my first sight of Malay seamen.'

10. *The captain* (p. 45). The master of the *Vidar* was one James Craig, an Englishman who had been appointed a year before Conrad joined the ship, and got on friendly terms with him.

11. *the second engineer* (p. 45). Following Jean-Aubry, Sherry (p. 31) assumes that this figure was modelled on John C. Niven, the *Vidar's* second engineer.

12. *Our chief engineer* (p. 45). Similarly, Sherry believes that his prototype was James Allen, the *Vidar's* first engineer. When Conrad signed on, both men had been four years with the ship, and were well informed about the Archipelago.

13. *the Harbour Office* (p. 46). The headquarters of the administration of maritime affairs in the Singapore region. This building, both inside and out, used to be essentially as Conrad described it (Sherry, pp. 176 and 196).

14. *punkahs* (p. 46). Large swinging fans made of cloth stretched on a rectangular frame suspended from the ceiling and worked by a cord.

15. *the Officers' Sailors' Home* (p. 47). The original compound, now the site of a cinema, contained two buildings, the Officers' Home and the

148

Sailors' Home, both for officers. Conrad is describing the latter (Sherry, p. 182). He stayed in the Sailors' Home for two weeks (4 January–19 January 1888).

16. *Chief Steward* (p. 47). While resident in the Sailors' Home, Conrad seems to have had a quarrel with its supervisor, one C. Phillips, 'an evangelist and temperance worker and an inspector of brothels' (Najder, p. 102). Of him Conrad wrote: 'The "Home" steward's name (in my time) I don't remember. He was a meagre, wizened creature, always bemoaning his fate, and did try to do me an unfriendly turn for some reason or other' (letter to W. G. St Clair, editor of the *Singapore Free Press*, 31 March 1917, quoted Sherry, p. 317).

17. *antimacassars* (p. 48). Coverings placed over the backs of sofas and armchairs as protection against stains from a brand of hair-oil known as macassar.

18. *Hamilton* (p. 49). Sherry (pp. 213–14) mentions a C. Hamilton, who was first mate of the S.S. *Martaban* in 1883, and who might have been offered the command of the *Otago* before Conrad. A Hamilton turns down a command in 'The End of the Tether' (Dent Collected Edition, p. 199): 'So I . . . sent word for Hamilton – the worst loafer of them all – and just made him go. Threatened to instruct the steward of the Sailors' Home to have him turned out neck and crop. He did not think the berth was good enough – if you – please.'

19. *Captain Giles* (p. 49). In his letter to St Clair (Sherry, p. 317) Conrad wrote: 'My Captain Giles was a man called Patterson, a dear, thick, dreary creature with an enormous reputation for knowledge of the Sulu Sea.' St Clair remembered him 'as a stout ungainly man often to be seen at Motion's, the chronometer and compass-regulating business in Battery Road' (from his article 'Two Interesting Letters' in the *Ceylon Observer*, reprinted in the *Malay Mail* of 2 September 1924).

20. *Solo Sea* (p. 49). A variant of Sulu Sea (see previous note), a square of ocean bounded by Borneo to the south-west, Palawan to the north-west, the Philippines to the north-east and the Sulu Islands to the south-east.

21. *tiffin-time* (p. 49). A light midday meal (from Anglo-Indian *tiff*, meaning 'to sip').

22. *Palawan* (p. 50). A 200-mile-long island, west of the Philippines, forming the north-west edge of the Sulu Sea.

23. *Queen Victoria's first jubilee celebrations* (p. 53). 1887.

24. *peon* (p. 55). A native attendant or messenger (from the Spanish for 'foot-soldier'; cf. 'police peon', p. 74).

25. *master attendant* (p. 56). Also known as the marine superintendent (p.

63), the official responsible for the general supervision of a colonial port and its shipping was also a marine magistrate, an inspector of lighthouses, etc. In 'The End of the Tether', Conrad defined his functions with complete accuracy: 'A master-attendant is a superior sort of harbour-master; a person, out in the East, of some consequence in his sphere; a Government official, a magistrate for the waters of the port, and possessed of a vast but ill-defined disciplinary authority over seamen of all classes' (Dent Collected Edition, p. 195). Captain Henry Ellis, the model for Conrad's Ellis, was born in Ireland in 1835, was appointed master attendant at Singapore in 1873, and retired almost immediately after interviewing Conrad for the *Otago* command – to be precise, six days before the latter's return from Bangkok. He died in 1908. The *Singapore Free Press* of 20 February 1908 described him as 'a strong official, blunt and straightforward, standing no nonsense, with a good deal of Irish humour about him and some national touchiness as well' (quoted Sherry, p. 200).

26. *coxswain* (p. 63). The helmsman of a boat (from 'cock', meaning 'ship's boat', and 'swain', meaning 'male servant').

27. *shipping-master* (p. 63). Official supervising the signing-on and discharging of seamen.

28. *Melita* (p. 66). Ellis's memorandum to Conrad has been preserved, and reads: 'This is to inform you that you are required to proceed to-day in the S.S. *Melita* to Bangkok and you will report your arrival to the British Consul and produce this memorandum which will show that I have engaged you to be Master of the *Otago* in accordance with the Consul's telegram' (quoted in Baines, p. 120). The voyage took four days.

29. *Bangkok* (p. 66). The capital of modern Thailand, formerly Siam, in Conrad's time almost entirely built on a complex of rafts, floating pontoons and piles at the edges of innumerable canals. Its chief exports were teak and rice.

CHAPTER TWO

1. *coolies* (p. 73). Native burden-carriers (from *Kuli*, the name of an Indian aboriginal tribe).

2. *stern-sheets* (p. 76). The internal stern portion of a boat (sometimes the aft flooring-boards or seats).

3. *the bar* (p. 78). A shallow bank of sand or silt across the mouth of a river or harbour. The bar across the entrance of the Menam River on which Bangkok is situated was only 14 feet below the surface,

though the 300-yard wide harbour was of a good depth up to both banks.

4. *bends* (p. 78). Bangkok is twenty miles upstream.

5. *pagoda* (p. 78). A Buddhist temple in pyramidal form. Bangkok is scattered with monasteries and temples with coloured tile roofs and gilded spires. The principal one, known as the Golden Mount, is over 400 feet high, forming the notable landmark to which Conrad refers.

6. *King's Palace* (p. 78). This rises on a bend of the river at the centre of the city. Enclosed by walls, it gives the appearance of a second city within the first.

7. *there she was* (p. 79). The *Otago* was a 367-ton barque (i.e. a three-masted vessel with fore- and mainmasts square-rigged, and mizzenmast fore-and-aft rigged), measuring 147 by 26 by 14 feet, built in Glasgow, and registered in Adelaide.

8. *balk* (p. 80) A roughly squared beam. The *Otago*'s first cargo under Conrad was indeed teak (Najder, p. 106).

9. *trucks* (p. 80). A cap of wood fixed to the head of a mast.

10. *companion-way* (p. 80). The stair*case* to the cabin, the entrance to which is protected by a wooden hood (or 'companion').

11. *lobby* (p. 81). The passageway in the forepart of the cabin.

CHAPTER THREE

1. *ormolu* (p. 82). Gold-coloured alloy, used in the decoration of furniture (from the French *or moulu*).

2. *bulkheads* (p. 82). Partitions. The master's cabin, which is frequently called a saloon in this text, is unusually grand.

3. *His name was Burns* (p. 83). The first mate of the *Otago* was called Charles Born. After the death of her captain off the southern coast of Cochin-China (Vietnam), he brought the ship into Bangkok. He was only three years older than Conrad; nor does he seem to have been laid up in port, at least not as seriously as his fictional counterpart. But he does seem to have envied Conrad's promotion, even though he was not yet formally qualified. He obtained his master's ticket in Melbourne, but failed to succeed Conrad, despite the latter's favourable recommendation. Conrad summed him up in *The Mirror of the Sea*: 'Upon the whole, I think he was one of the most uncomfortable shipmates possible for a young commander. If it is permissible to criticise the absent, I should say he had a little too much of the sense of insecurity which is so invaluable in a seaman. He had an extremely disturbing air of being everlastingly ready (even

when seated at table at my right hand before a plate of salt beef) to grapple with some impending calamity. I must hasten to add that he had also the other qualification necessary to make a trustworthy seaman – that of absolute confidence in himself. What was really wrong with him is that he had these qualities in an unrestful degree. His eternally watchful demeanour, his jerky, nervous talk, even his, as it were, determined silences, seemed to imply – and, I believe, they did imply – that to his mind the ship was never safe in my hands' (Dent Collected Edition, pp. 18–19).

4. *dégagé* (p. 84). Detached, carefree.

5. *The last captain* (p. 85). Conrad's predecessor on the *Otago* was Captain John Snadden. Having docked in Haiphong on 29 October 1887 with a cargo of coal from Newcastle, Australia, he departed for Hong Kong on 22 November. He was taken ill at sea with heart disease. On 5 December, he dictated to Born a letter of farewell to his family, making practical arrangements (he was part-owner of the *Otago*) and expressing gratitude towards Born. This letter was duly sent, and a fragment of it has survived. He died on 8 December, and was buried at sea probably off Cap St Jacques (i.e. at a considerable distance from the entrance to the Gulf of Siam). Sherry (p. 223) holds that he was very unlikely to have been either negligent or dilatory. He – or a version of him – also makes an appearance in 'Falk' (Dent Collected Edition, pp. 153–4).

6. *rudder-casing* (p. 85). The cabin being aft, under the poop deck, the rudder projects somewhat into the cabin space.

7. *seven bells in the forenoon watch* (p. 85). A watch is a four-hour duty period, divided by bells at half-hour intervals. 'Seven bells' is therefore half an hour before the end of the watch.

8. *sextant* (p. 86). An astronomical instrument, shaped like a segment of a circle, and furnished with a graduated arc of a sixth of a circle, for measuring the altitude of celestial bodies in order to determine the latitude.

9. *Haiphong* (p. 87). The principal seaport of what is now known as North Vietnam, on the Red River delta, about forty miles from Hanoi.

10. *Hong-Kong* (p. 88). This famous locality is no more than 482 miles from Haiphong, nor are 'fierce monsoons' expected in the season in which Snadden set his course for Hong Kong.

11. *put the helm up* (p. 88). The order to place the helm (or wheel, tiller) so as to bring the rudder to leeward (away from the wind), as opposed to 'down helm', the order to bring the rudder to windward.

12. *Pulo Condor* (p. 89). These are the Iles de Paulo Condore, off the

southernmost point of modern South Vietnam, the key navigational target for ships rounding the Cochin-China peninsula.

13. *telegraph cable* (p. 91). The cable between Singapore and Bangkok was laid in about 1882.

14. *charter-party* (p. 92). The deed made between ship-owners and merchants for the hire of a ship and the safe delivery of its cargo.

15. *the doctor of our Legation* (p. 93). William Willis, the doctor of the British consulate to Siam, supplied Conrad with the following letter, dated February 1888: 'I think it is not out of place on my part that I should state, though not asked by you to do so, to prevent any misapprehension hereafter, that the crew of the sailing ship *Otago* has suffered severely whilst in Bangkok from tropical diseases, including fever, dysentery and cholera; and I can speak of my own knowledge, that you have done all in your power in the trying and responsible position of Master of the Ship to hasten the departure of your vessel from this unhealthy place and at the same time to save the lives of the men under your command' (Baines, p. 122).

16. *The men ailed* (p. 93). The *Otago's* complement, when it sailed from Bangkok, totalled nine: the captain (originally Polish), two officers (Born, a German, and Jackson, an Englishman), and six sailors (two Englishmen, two Norwegians, one Scot, and one German). When he reached Singapore, Conrad had to replace four sailors. Presuming that the remaining two had not been unaffected by fever, we must conclude that *The Shadow-Line* does not exaggerate his plight as much as it is generally claimed.

17. *He was taken ashore . . . and died there* (p. 93). One John Carlson, cook and steward of the *Otago*, died of cholera in Bangkok Hospital on 16 January 1888, six days before Conrad's arrival. Sherry suggests (p. 231) that Carlson begged to be allowed to remain on board, and that Conrad, who heard this story when he joined the ship, simply transferred it to Burns. Evidence suggests strongly that this seaman could not be replaced.

18. *Ransome was the cook* (p. 94). One Pat Conway, an able seaman, was, like Ransome, the last to leave the ship when it anchored at Singapore. He was too ill to sign his name, but got paid higher wages. Sherry thinks that this may have been because he was obliged to combine the seaman's duties with those of cook and steward. Najder (p. 521) points out that the higher pay was due to his status as able seaman (a rank above that of ordinary seaman), and doubts that he served as a model for Ransome.

19. *gharry* (p. 95). A horse-drawn vehicle resembling a bathing machine (Anglo-Indian).

20. *starboard spare cabin* (p. 96). Clearly there are two cabins, in addition to the 'saloon'; an inner cabin on the starboard side (right, facing forward) and a cabin opening on the lobby on the port side (left, facing forward).

21. *quarter-deck* (p. 98). That quarter of the upper deck between the stern and the after-mast.

22. *shore-fasts* (p. 98). Ropes attaching the vessel to the quay.

23. *poop* (p. 98). The raised deck at the stern of the ship containing the accommodation of the ship's officers, and from which the ship is steered and directed.

24. *the second officer* (p. 98). When Conrad took over the *Otago*, the second mate was a man called Jackson; when Conrad resigned two years later, this officer had been replaced by one F. Totterman. In 'Falk', Conrad writes: '. . . his name was Tottersen, or something like that. His practice was to wear on his head, in that tropical climate, a mangy fur cap. He was, without exception, the stupidest man I have ever seen on board ship. And he looked it too. He looked so confoundedly stupid that it was a matter of surprise for me when he answered to his name' (Dent Collected Edition, p. 178). In *The Shadow-Line* it looks as if Conrad was remembering the latter.

25. *the anchor-watch man* (p. 99). The anchor watch is that part of the crew kept on duty while the ship is at anchor.

26. *bulkhead-lamp* (p. 99). The oil-lamp attached to the bulkhead or partition.

27. *windlass* (p. 100). A machine with a barrel revolving horizontally to the deck for weighing the anchor.

28. *trimmed the yards* (p. 100). i.e. adjusted the spars supporting the sails with reference to the wind's direction and the ship's course.

CHAPTER FOUR

1. *port bow* (p. 102). The left side, facing forward, of the rounded fore-end of the ship (here south-east, since the ship is travelling south).

2. *Cape Liant* (p. 102). At its head, the Gulf of Siam narrows to a square area of sea called the Bight of Bangkok. Cape Liant marks the southeast corner of the Bight.

3. *The Island of Koh-ring* (p. 107). The eastern edge of the Gulf of Siam is dotted with innumerable islands. In the northern section (off the coast of modern Cambodia) the names are prefixed with the particle 'Ko', in the southern (off modern Vietnam) with the particle 'Kas'. Conrad's island, which had already featured at the climax of 'The Secret Sharer',

is almost certainly fictitious, but it can safely be imagined as located in the far north-eastern corner of the Gulf.

4. *braces* (p. 110). Ropes attached to the yards for trimming the sails (see note above for *trimmed the yards*).

CHAPTER FIVE

1. *with their crews all dead* (p. 113). Such incidents were part of the storytelling repertoire of seamen, and found their archetype in the legend of the Flying Dutchman (mentioned on p. 115), a spectral ship seen in stormy weather usually off the Cape of Good Hope. According to Walter Scott, it was originally a vessel cursed by a dreadful murder and an outbreak of the plague, which closed every port against it and condemned it to an eternity of wandering. Equally plausible as a source were the blind peregrinations of ships that had missed a remote island destination in the days before the discovery of the longitude (mid eighteenth century). The writing of *The Shadow-Line* sometimes echoes, or half echoes, phrases from *Hamlet* (listed by Hawthorn in his recent edition) or from Coleridge's *The Ancient Mariner* (audible to the first reviewers). But in my opinion, attempts to treat these allusions as interpretative signals, instead of textural enrichments, are misconceived, for they encourage critics to locate such notions as guilt, redemption and the supernatural in an inappropriate interpretative space. Readers hungry for intertextual indices (to use the current critical lingo) might more profitably meditate on the explicit allusion to Baudelaire's 'La Musique'.

2. *Tongkin* (p. 115). More usually 'Tongking' or 'Tonkin', it is the name of the north-eastern province of Vietnam, containing Hanoi and Haiphong.

3. *all aback* (p. 119). With sails laid back against the masts.

4. *cleat ... belaying pin ... ring-bolt* (p. 119). A cleat is an anvil-shaped piece of wood or iron bolted down for securing ropes; a belaying pin is a short, solid cylinder of wood or iron secured into a socket for belaying (i.e. fixing a running rope); and a ring-bolt is a bolt with an eye at one end, through which a ring is inserted.

5. *Frenchy* (p. 120). There was no Frenchman in the crew of the *Otago*, and not even Sherry has been able to propose a prototype.

6. *Gambril* (p. 120). No member of the crew of the *Otago* was old enough to serve as a model for him. According to Hawthorn (ed. cit.) Conrad's manuscript names him as Smith. A Gambril features in 'Falk'.

7. *binnacle* (p. 123). A receptacle for a ship's compass, fitted with a binnacle lamp and mounted on a binnacle stand.

8. *Meinam* (p. 125). Often spelt 'Menam'; see note for p. 78, above, for *the bar*.

9. *bend another suit* (p. 125). To 'bend' is to tie or fasten a sail; a 'suit' is the whole set of sails for a ship, or for a mast, or even (as in this case) for a spar.

10. *mainsail* (p. 127). The lowest sail on the mainmast, and hence the largest sail on the ship.

11. *leech-line* (p. 127). A rope attached to the 'leech', or perpendicular side of a square sail, used for furling it.

12. *capstan* (p. 127). A barrel revolving on an axis vertical to the deck, with bars inserted horizontally into sockets at its head, pushed by men walking round to hoist heavy spars or sails.

13. *square the mainyard* (p. 127). Set it at right angles to the keel of the ship.

CHAPTER SIX

1. *helm . . . amidships* (p. 128). With the rudder set directly towards the middle of the ship, i.e. in line with the keel.

2. *halyards* (p. 129). Ropes used for raising or lowering a sail or a yard.

3. *running* (p. 129). Capable of moving easily when pulled.

4. *sternway* (p. 129). The pressure on the rudder caused by the ship's movement.

5. *break of the poop* (p. 132). The fore-partition of the poop, where it drops to meet the main deck.

6. *scuppers* (p. 132). Holes in a ship's sides, to carry off water from the decks.

7. *lubber* (p. 132). Clumsy seaman.

8. *chain sheet* (p. 133). A metal contrivance of linked elements used to carry the corners of the sails beyond the ship's sides.

9. *run of the sea* (p. 133). Movement of the water in a regular direction.

10. *roads* (p. 134). Sheltered piece of water near the shore or harbour, where ships can anchor in safety.

11. *after-grating* (p. 138). The open woodwork cover for the aft hatchway.

12. *to slat* (p. 139). To flap violently.

13. *mizzenmast* (p. 139). Rear mast.

14. *anchors cock-billed* (p. 140). With the anchor-bill (the points of the flukes) cocked (pointing upwards), the anchor hangs from the cat-head ready for dropping.

15. *compressors* (p. 140). Iron levers for braking the chain cable (or anchor cable) as it runs out.

16. *various men-of-war* (p. 141). There were five warships in harbour when the *Otago* reached Singapore.

17. *at least five naval surgeons* (p. 141). A joke against the blood-thirstiness of the surgical profession. The *Otago* took three weeks to negotiate the 800-mile passage from Bangkok to Singapore. On arrival it showed a signal for medical assistance. According to a report in the *Singapore Free Press* of 2 March 1888: 'The British bark *Otago*, bound from Bangkok to Sydney with a cargo of rice [*sic*], put into port here last evening for medical ad── as several of the crew are suffering from fever and the Captain wished to get a further supply of medicine before he proceeded on his journey. Dr Mugliston went on board and ordered three [*sic*] of the crew to be sent to Hospital. The vessel is outside the Harbour limits' (quoted Sherry, p. 257). As we have already noted, a fourth seaman left the ship at the last minute.

18. *steam-pinnace* (p. 141). A double-banked boat forming part of the equipment of a man-of-war.

19. *bluejackets* (p. 141). Sailors on a warship, as opposed to marines (i.e. soldiers).

20. *let me off the port dues* (p. 143). In his letter to St Clair (op. cit.) Conrad wrote: 'Yes, I remember Bradbury. It was he who let me off port-dues when I put into Singapore in distress with *all* my crew unfit for duty (1888)' (quoted Sherry, p. 316).

21. *shipwrecked crew* (p. 143). The *Otago* took on five men in Singapore, four to replace the hospitalized men, one to replace the dead cook–steward Carlson (see note for p. 93, above, for *He was taken ashore . . .*). Only one of these came from the crew of the recently shipwrecked *Anne Millicent*; the others came from three other ships (Najder, pp. 106 and 521).

22. *be off . . . tomorrow* (p. 145). The *Otago* stayed in Singapore for three days only, leaving on 3 March, bound for Sydney.

FOR THE BEST IN PAPERBACKS, LOOK FOR THE

In every corner of the world, on every subject under the sun, Penguin represents quality and variety – the very best in publishing today.

For complete information about books available from Penguin – including Pelicans, Puffins, Peregrines and Penguin Classics – and how to order them, write to us at the appropriate address below. Please note that for copyright reasons the selection of books varies from country to country.

In the United Kingdom: For a complete list of books available from Penguin in the U.K., please write to *Dept E.P., Penguin Books Ltd, Harmondsworth, Middlesex, UB7 0DA*

In the United States: For a complete list of books available from Penguin in the U.S., please write to *Dept BA, Penguin, 299 Murray Hill Parkway, East Rutherford, New Jersey 07073*

In Canada: For a complete list of books available from Penguin in Canada, please write to *Penguin Books Canada Ltd, 2801 John Street, Markham, Ontario L3R 1B4*

In Australia: For a complete list of books available from Penguin in Australia, please write to the *Marketing Department, Penguin Books Australia Ltd, P.O. Box 257, Ringwood, Victoria 3134*

In New Zealand: For a complete list of books available from Penguin in New Zealand, please write to the *Marketing Department, Penguin Books (NZ) Ltd, Private Bag, Takapuna, Auckland 9*

In India: For a complete list of books available from Penguin, please write to *Penguin Overseas Ltd, 706 Eros Apartments, 56 Nehru Place, New Delhi, 110019*

In Holland: For a complete list of books available from Penguin in Holland, please write to *Penguin Books Nederland B.V., Postbus 195, NL–1380AD Weesp, Netherlands*

In Germany: For a complete list of books available from Penguin, please write to *Penguin Books Ltd, Friedrichstrasse 10 – 12, D–6000 Frankfurt Main 1, Federal Republic of Germany*

In Spain: For a complete list of books available from Penguin in Spain, please write to *Longman Penguin España, Calle San Nicolas 15, E–28013 Madrid, Spain*